The Word

Tales from a Revolution: Maryland

Also by Lars D. H. Hedbor,
available from Brief Candle Press:

The Prize: Tales From a Revolution - Vermont
The Light: Tales From a Revolution - New-Jersey
The Smoke: Tales From a Revolution - New-York
The Declaration: Tales From a Revolution - South-Carolina
The Break: Tales From a Revolution - Nova-Scotia
The Wind: Tales From a Revolution - West-Florida
The Darkness: Tales From a Revolution - Maine
The Path: Tales From a Revolution - Rhode-Island
The Freedman: Tales From a Revolution - North-Carolina
The Tree: Tales From a Revolution - New-Hampshire
The Mine: Tales From a Revolution - Connecticut
The Siege: Tales From a Revolution - Virginia
The Will: Tales From a Revolution - Pennsylvania
The Convention: Tales From a Revolution - Massachusetts
The Oath: Tales From a Revolution - Georgia
The Powder: Tales From a Revolution - Bermuda

The Word

Lars D. H. Hedbor

Brief Candle
Press

Cover and book design: Brief Candle Press.
Cover image based on "Westphalia," Albert Bierstadt, 1855.
Map reproduction courtesy of Library of Congress, Geography and Map Division.
Fonts: Allegheney, Doves Type, and IM FELL English.

First Brief Candle Press edition published 2024.
www.briefcandlepress.com

ISBN: 978-1-942319-84-9

Dedication

*To all those who strive
to follow the principles of
love, respect, and care
for their fellow man*

PHILADELPHIA
Newcastle
Wilmington
DELAWARE BAY
DELAWARE COUNTIES
Dover
Lewes
Chester
MARYLAND
YORK
Baltimore
Georgetown
Nottingham
Kings berry
Frederick
Annapolis
Bladensburg
Georgetown
Alexandria
Belhaven
Colchester
Marlboro
Piscatawa
Oxford
Cambridge
Queens Town
The Meadows
Ft. Cumberland
Harpers Fer.
Winchester or Frederick T.
Ld. Fairfax's
Chester's
Fredericksburg
Orange
Hanover
Goochland
Newcastle
James
Westham
Quantico
New Marlboro
Germanna
Court House
Louisa
South Anna R.
North Anna R.
Rapanna R.
Rapidanna R.
Tappahannock
Pamunky R.
Mattapanay R.
Potowmack R.
Potowmack R.
CHESAPEAK
VIRGINIA
MARYLAND
Three Forks
Rays T.
Fr. Ann R.
Walkers
Washington
Nantue
Pocomoke
Somerset
Wicomoco
Matomkin
Matsapreak
Teches
Matchapungo
North Branch
South Branch
Capecapon R.
Peaked Ridge
North M. or Blue Ridge
Great Mts.
Jacksons R.
Raccoon Ch.
Salem
Greenwich
Eggl.
False C.
Rehob.
Indian R.
Fenw.
Cedar Swamp
Watkins
Hanover
Deer C.
Ramsey
S. Mary's
Leeds
Nominy
Yeocomico
Cinquack
Watts Isd.
Windmill Pt.
Indian c.
Powels

Chapter I

It was a rainy Tuesday afternoon when God first spoke to Prosper Creale. The smell of the last season's thawing manure rose from the field around him, almost thick enough to see, and Prosper was pondering whether the mud that pulled at his boots would nourish the precious, hoarded seed stock, when he heard a clear, firm voice in his ear.

"Unto whomsoever much is given, of him shall be much required."

Prosper whirled around, looking for whatever prankster had crept up on him to quote Scripture with no context. He stood alone, surrounded by ten open acres or more of unplowed soil, broken up only by rivulets of water, refreshed by another band of rain that swept over the field toward him.

His eyes narrowed, and a deep frown came over his face, creasing the early-developing lines between his eyebrows. He had heard about people who heard voices from nowhere, and he didn't particularly want to find himself in their company.

Still, the voice had been as distinct as though spoken from the pulpit of a meeting-house, and the statement had been akin to the sort of thing that the new preacher, Mister Garrettson, would have begun a meeting with.

It hadn't been Mister Garrettson's voice, though, even if that worthy man could somehow have projected his words into

Prosper's ear. Scowling again, he started to trudge back to the house, having come to the decision that he would have his field hands proceed with plowing and planting.

"You have been given much. What will you render unto those who most deserve it?"

The voice was, if anything, even clearer now, and Prosper felt panic creeping over him as he cast about again in vain to discover its source. He felt rising anger, too, at what seemed to him to be the voice's mocking of his circumstances.

If a stretch of muddy, reeking farmland marked him as having been given so much, then why was he struggling so to keep up with the expenses of eking out a living from the reluctant earth? Rumors of war with the mother country had grown from the grumblings of men deep in their cups at the tavern into open conflict up in Massachusetts-Bay and on down into the colonies to the south of Maryland, but Prosper's name had seemed to be a taunt even before that.

While other men around him had been fortunate in the article of acquiring good hands to work their land, Prosper had no more than three upon whom he could rely, and was weighed down with another dozen who had to be hectored into performing the most basic of their responsibilities.

One of his boots nearly slid off his foot as he stepped out of a particularly sticky patch of mud, and he snorted to himself. The land itself required his constant attention and wariness, lest it strip him even of his clothing.

No, the only thing he had been blessed with plenty of was children, each of them yet another mouth to feed at a table that was ever more crowded.

And now, it appeared, he was to lose his sanity, on top of everything else. He shook his head, then, sharply remembering the testimony that the preacher Mister Garrettson had shared a month prior at a meeting called together by a neighbor.

"One day, being at some distance from home, I encountered a zealous exhorter of the Methodists. He asked me plainly if I were born again, and I told him that I had some reason to hope that I was. The man asked me if I knew that my sins were forgiven."

Mister Garrettson had paused to take a sip of water, then continued in a low, serious tone. "I told the exhorter that I did not know that, nor did I expect that knowledge in this world. The Methodist gave me a mournful look and told me that he perceived that I was on the broad road to hell, and that if I were to die in this state, I would be damned."

The preacher looked out at the meeting, shaking his head in recalled wonder. "I told this man that the Scripture tells us that the tree is known by its fruit, and that our Lord condemns rash judgment of our fellow man. I demanded of him what he knew of my life that induced him to pass judgment on me in such a manner. I did not wait for his answer, but said only that I pitied him, and turned my back on him."

After taking another drink from his cup, Mister Garrettson continued, "However, I could not easily forget the words of that pious young man, for in fact, they were like spears running me through where I stood. Even though I had heaped abuse on him for saying them, there was some part of me that recognized the truth in what he had said."

The men around Prosper in the impromptu meeting-house sat as rapt as he was himself as they waited for the preacher to continue.

"I continued in this state until one day last June. That blessed morning I shall never forget! The prior night, I had gone to bed as usual, and slept until the break of day. Just as I awoke, though, I was greatly alarmed to hear an awful voice, which said, 'Awake, sinner, for you are not prepared to die.' It was as loud as thunder, yet the panes of my window did not rattle. This was the voice of our Lord, given directly into my ear, and audible to none other."

Prosper considered this testimony now, as he stood in the muddy field, and wondered if he had been blessed with a similar experience. He wasn't sure that possibility was any less distressing than simply having his own mind play tricks on him. Someone who had a direct encounter with God Himself could hardly claim that he had not been given much, after all, regardless of his worldly circumstances.

Whatever the case was, he still had a crop to get put in, and a family to feed. The state of his sanity — and his soul, were that in question — must wait for another day.

He reached the house just as the rain stopped, and he shook his head again at the irony of it. If the Lord were trying to speak to him, it seemed as though He could have chosen to be more gentle about it. The impious thought made him frown at himself now, as he drew off his filthy boots at the door to avoid tracking more muck into the house.

Hearing Prosper close the door, Kristine called out, "Mind that you get out of your wet things straight away, husband. I've a warm cup ready for you, and your second-best shirt is hanging there dry by the door."

The care that his wife's preparations showed for him warmed Prosper's heart, and he added a good helpmeet to the list of the many things he'd been given.

"I thank you, wife, and I will gladly come for that cup as soon as I am dry," he called back to her, and busied himself with changing. His breeches would need washing — no matter how carefully he walked, the mud of the fields inevitably seemed to reach out to spatter them — but his wet shirt looked as though it would be fine as soon as it was dry.

Gratefully, he slipped his head into the fresh shirt, its dry warmth enveloping him down to his knees, and padded in to the kitchen. Kristine nodded to acknowledge his appearance, and motioned with her chin to the steaming cup on the table.

Lifting it to his mouth and sniffing it, Prosper was happy to detect that while it wasn't a proper flip, it was still fortified with at least a splash of the whiskey he'd brought home to replace the ever more expensive rum he'd once favored. The warmth of the drink flooded into his gut as he drank, and he smiled at his wife.

"Even though I got myself rained upon, the visit to the field was worthwhile. I will have Prince get the men out there tomorrow, if the weather permits."

Kristine nodded absently, more focused on stirring the pot of stew she had over the fire than on the details of what her husband was telling her. The twins seemed to be whispering secrets to one another where they sat in the next room, though they were supposed to be practicing their needlework.

"There is no danger of frost, naturally, though it is cold enough to still be unpleasant in the rain. More importantly, I believe that the good dung that we secured from Wrangel last year has had enough time to age and provide sustenance to a new crop."

He continued to describe to her how he intended to have the field plowed, and how much of his seed stores he would risk in the planting, but he could tell that her mind was otherwise occupied.

Abruptly, she said, "Tace is running a fever."

Prosper answered dismissively, "Isn't that what children do, when they're not clearing out the root cellar or raising a fuss with the neighbor's livestock?" He glanced over at the girls, hopeful that they hadn't taken offense, but they were still giggling behind their hands at some private amusement.

Kristine pursed her lips at him, and Prosper knew that he'd said the wrong thing. He held up his hands to forestall her angry words. "Is there aught that we can do for her?"

"I used the last of the feverfew on Phillip a fortnight ago. Can you get me some more?"

Prosper sighed. "I already owe Missus Grant more than three shillings for what we've needed this winter. I do not know where we will get the money to satisfy the debt, but I will pay her a visit tomorrow."

"Tace's fever has been getting worse all day, husband."

Prosper listened for the rain on the roof and heard nothing but some lingering dripping outside from the eaves. He nodded and raised his cup. "I will set out as soon as I've finished this. Are my other breeches fit to wear, or should I put back on my muddy ones?"

"I'll put your breeches up by the fire to warm them," she replied. "They're likely cleaner than the ones you were wearing, and they're certainly drier."

He nodded, but said nothing, instead slurping noisily at

the drink as she swung the pot off the fire and fetched the clothes, draping them over a stool before the hearth.

Prosper lost himself in thought, his usual unconscious grimace settling across his face. That Grant woman was not someone he relished having to deal with, but he knew that he'd have no peace until little Tace had her remedy, and her fever had broken.

Missus Grant was one of those people whom one tolerated, rather than relished, and Prosper couldn't quite say whether it was because of her knack of seeing too much of the truth behind things, or her inclination to presume that she could do so in all cases.

After their third son, Phillip, was born, Kristine had sent him for an herb she said she needed for her own relief, and the medicine woman had given him a knowing look as he repeated the carefully memorized name.

"Your wife has had enough of children, has she?"

Prosper frowned in confusion, and Missus Grant waved a dismissive hand. "Never you mind, Mister Creale. 'Tis women's affairs, and you are no more than the courier, I see." Turning to her closely packed shelves, she'd plucked down a small bag and handed it to him, naming the price.

As Prosper had handed over a creased and worn-looking bill, the woman had sighed, accepting it, and added, "I presume the Missus Creale knows well enough how to prepare this, but if not, she can send you back for the instructions. As I recall, she reads well enough."

"She can read the word of God on Sundays, and that's all she needs," Prosper had retorted. In fact, his wife had a better knack of reading than he did, and their family Bible — purchased in a more successful year — was more likely to be in her hands during their devotions than his. It rankled, but though he struggled to make sense of the words on the page, he had no trouble instructing the children once she had provided the reading.

It helped that what he did hear, he could recall relatively easily, and together with what he heard preachers say about the passages they based their teachings on, he felt more than equal to the responsibility of bringing up his children with a proper regard for their Lord.

Whatever "women's affairs" had been in the bag he'd brought back to his wife, there had been no more children in several years, and though he said nothing of it to Kristine, he was relieved enough to have no new mouths to feed, at least.

Frowning to himself yet again, he tossed back the last of the fortified warm milk and rose from the table. Pulling on his breeches, he nodded to his wife and stepped back into his chilled boots at the door, adding his woolen cape over his shoulders for warmth.

The afternoon had turned brisk, and though no more rain sheeted down, clouds skimmed overhead, looking near enough that a taller man might think of stretching up to touch them. A treeline spoiled the illusion — the clouds easily cleared the highest branches — but the winds that propelled them so quickly overhead gusted nearer the ground, too, adding to the chill in the air.

He had just set off on the road into the village when the same voice from nowhere spoke into his ear for the last time that day, saying only, "Your gifts are not for your use alone."

Prosper stopped dead in the road, and glared around him, as though daring the speaker to show himself, but when he found nothing more suspicious than a cat slinking into the slaves' quarters, he shook his head and continued on his way.

Chapter 2

Missus Grant looked up as Prosper entered her little shop, greeting him with, "You look more sour than usual, Mister Creale. Does something more than the late spring trouble you?"

Of all the people whom Prosper knew, Missus Grant was pretty close to the last one to whom he would confess his strange experiences of the day. "I am worried about my daughter Tace, madame. My wife has sent me to replenish her supply of feverfew for the child."

"A sick daughter is certainly reason enough to worry, but I have seen you before when your wife was tending one or another of your children, and yet your manner is not usually so powerfully grim." She gazed directly at him with narrowed eyes, and Prosper could almost feel her rooting through the unspoken secrets of his innermost thoughts.

He broke eye contact with her, and although he wouldn't acknowledge that she'd made him uncomfortable, he also would not tolerate her continuing to do so.

Dismissively, he said only, "I've many things on my mind, Missus Grant, and much to do before the day is out." He fished into his purse and pulled out a pitiful handful of coins.

He could see her eyes dart to the sound of the dull clink in his hand, but he said only, "This is all I have to offer you. Missus

Creale begs that you provide as much of the herb as it will pay for." He spread the coins out on the tabletop between them.

She glanced over them and fetched another of her ubiquitous little bags. "This ought to last the rest of the spring, at least, so long as the summer fevers remain at bay." She placed the bag onto the table, her other hand sweeping the coins away into her own purse.

"You still appear troubled, Mister Creale. Is there some ailment that you are reluctant to name to me? I assure you, your private details remain between us, as a matter of my duty to my customers."

Prosper shook his head firmly, without hesitation. "Nay, Missus Grant, I am but worried about the late start to the season, whether my hands will do their duty, and whether the crop that has sustained my family for so many years is still the right one for my land. More than that, whether the troublemakers in Massachusetts-Bay will bring all to ruin by inviting the horrors of battle to our doors."

He gave her a sardonic half-smile. "There are plenty of matters beyond the everyday occurrence of a child with a fever to trouble my mind, as you may imagine."

She inclined her head in acknowledgment. "I have no need to imagine. I know all too well that the disruptions imposed upon our trade have left us with no reliable source for many necessary articles of everyday living, to say nothing of the sorts of materials for which I must find sources."

She grimaced. "If the Royal Navy should happen to impose a fresh blockade upon our ports, there are many of the items I offer that will become nearly impossible to lay hands upon, at any price.

As it is, I have had no choice but to increase the prices I must charge for many things."

Shaking her head, she said, "I know you understand these matters, for you do not complain when your shilling buys less of one herb or another that your wife requires, but you would scarcely believe the abuse that is heaped upon my head by some in this community."

Prosper gave her a more appraising, respectful look. "I will confess that I have grumbled to Missus Creale from time to time about the costs her orders have, but I am sorry indeed to hear that there are those among us who would speak ill to a widow for that which you cannot control."

The herbalist gestured with her hands, motioning the hopelessness of the situation. "In troubled times, anyone who is at all different may be seen as a threat. I do not blame those who see me thus, but I do appreciate those such as yourself who at least keep the worst of their thoughts to themselves."

Prosper felt a flash of guilt for the uncharitable thoughts he had indulged in about the woman, and once again, he almost felt as though she could see the thoughts that swam through his mind.

She gave him a wry smile. "I do not deny that I am somewhat different. Ever since Mister Grant departed from this world, I have had no choice but to pursue a different path than most. I will not find another husband at my advanced age, and the typical options of going into service in some household as a washerwoman or cook's assistant hold no charms for me."

She shrugged and gathered in the contents of her shop with a sweep of her eyes. "So, I apply what my mother taught me when I was but a girl, as well as what I can learn of modern physic, and hope to do some good in my part of the world."

Prosper didn't know quite what moved him to say, "You do more than your share of good, Missus Grant, and our community is fortunate to benefit from your knowledge." It seemed the right thing to say, but it was not in his usual character.

She seemed to be aware of this herself, because she gave him a strange, suspicious glance for a moment before nodding in acknowledgment. "'Tis kind of you to say so." She gestured to the bag in his hand, adding, "You had best hurry that home to your child, then, so that it can do her more good than it will while we gossip."

He bowed his farewell, slipping out of the shop before anything more uncomfortable yet could pass through his lips. As he walked back home, his customary expression returned. What had moved him to speak so? In truth, he had no particular liking for the widow, nor did it benefit him to provide her with comforting words. He knew she would sell him what his wife asked for, and would continue to advise Kristine on how to use her wares to see to the health of their family, regardless of whether she felt he appreciated her.

He caught himself almost wishing that the voice from nowhere would return to give him some insight into his own actions, but it was, for the moment at least, silent.

His belly, however, was not so quiet, and its grumbling reminded him that he'd had nothing but a heel of bread since waking that morning. The thought of the stew that Kristine was tending over the fire sped his steps back toward home.

Glancing up, he saw that the clouds were still scudding overhead, propelled by winds that now barely reached the ground.

The tops of the taller trees alongside the road sometimes swayed under a gust aloft, but only an uneasy, fitful breeze pulled at his cape.

The sun briefly broke through a gap in the clouds, a ray of light pointing the way back toward his home, and Prosper increased his pace again. Was God still communicating with him, only now forsaking words and relying solely on signs?

He shook his head derisively at his own hubris in thinking that God would take the time to speak to a struggling farmer, or to arrange signs for such a figure of obscurity as himself. Men who were sharing the Gospel, who were out in the world, saving the souls of their neighbors, they might be worthy of God's individual attention, but a plain fellow like himself? Absurd.

Still, as he hurried along the road, Prosper was aware of a growing sense that he was being watched. He was well clear of the village, and no houses lay out along this way until Wrangell's place. Only the lonely road stretched out before him, lined with trees and fence-rows.

Looking at the aging split-rail fences, he was reminded of the lurid stories he'd heard of the engagement in Massachusetts the year prior, where the rebellious militia men had bragged of hiding behind fences to hunt the King's soldiers like so many dogs as they ran back to their garrison near Boston.

Was there some man concealed among the fence-rows here with a musket primed and waiting, considering whether the figure on the road was friend or foe? Prosper examined his surroundings minutely, even as he strove to give the appearance of merely being concerned for the weather.

If only he could persuade his heart that the danger he

imagined was only a phantasm, and not based on any actual evidence of his senses. He could feel it speeding up and starting to pound within his chest, responding to a fear that some part of his rational mind knew was unfounded.

The sharp sound of a shot rang out behind him then over the creaking and rustling of the trees, and he was in flight for his life before he had fully understood what he'd heard.

An odd crashing noise followed it, and he glanced over his shoulder to see what was happening behind him. At once, he understood that he had been spooked by nothing more dangerous than a tree snapped by a gust, falling across the road he had just passed over. While it might have presented some danger to him, it was nothing to fly from, and he stopped to catch his breath, leaning his hands onto his knees as laughter bubbled up and consumed him.

What a fellow he was, running from a dead tree, and conjuring up hostile gunmen on a road where he was the only person in sight. As his self-ridiculing chortles finally trailed off, he rose to his full height, a breeze drawing the cape out to billow behind him, and he turned back toward home, his mood lightened, and no longer sensing any unfriendly eye upon him.

Indeed, he was glad that there had been nobody to witness his embarrassment. He would have to come back to clear the road, but it could easily wait until the following day. In the meantime, his daughter was depending upon him to get home quickly, and he'd wasted enough time bantering with Missus Grant.

Entering his house, his stomach gurgled again at the rich aroma of the finished stew. After hanging his cape and removing his boots, he made his way into the kitchen, where Kristine was cradling Tace and spooning stew into the child's mouth.

Prosper smiled to see his daughter's solemn eyes wide and attentive, though he noticed that they lay in dark shadows under her pale forehead. Kristine looked up then, and said quietly, "I trust that you have the physic for her?"

"Aye," Prosper answered, pulling the sack from his purse and offering it to her.

She shook her head sharply, saying, "I cannot take it at this moment. Can you fill the kettle and get the water heating to make her a draught from it?"

Prosper said nothing, but set Missus Grant's sack on the table and turned to the task his wife had set him to. He knew that he ought to be irritated at being ordered to do her bidding in the kitchen, but where one of the children's welfare was at stake, he could easily enough tolerate it.

He dipped some water out of the pail beside the hearth, wishing yet again that he had the means to have help in the house for Kristine. She insisted that she didn't need him to incur the cost of purchasing a mere house slave, but at times like this, he knew that another pair of hands around the kitchen would make life far easier for the whole family.

The crane stuck as he swiveled it to suspend the kettle over the fire, and some of the water sloshed out to hiss on the coals, leaving behind a dead spot in the middle of the flames.

Kristine said nothing, but he could see her lips purse with displeasure. Stirring the coals with a poker, he added a couple of fresh sticks of wood to the fire. He smiled to himself with satisfaction as the evidence of his clumsiness disappeared behind a shower of sparks, and the flames eagerly spread along the rough grain of the split wood.

He noticed that the wood bin was less than half full, and made a mental note to ask Clement and Humility to bring more firewood in. His older sons were not the most dependable about noticing work that needed doing, but at least they would jump to a task that was pointed out to them.

Prosper returned to the table and busied himself with opening the sack. Missus Grant had used a coarse string to secure it, and the knot required coaxing before it finally loosened. By the time he got the sack opened, the water in the kettle was already starting to steam.

The herb released a sharp, bitter odor into the air of the kitchen, and Prosper wrinkled his nose at it.

He held the open bag up to Kristine's view. "How much should I use?"

She sighed and thought for a moment, glancing over to the kettle to judge how much water he'd added to it.

"Perhaps half a handful," she finally answered. "It smells as though it is still quite nearly as strong as when Missus Grant gathered it, so that is encouraging."

Tace sat up and looked over to see what Prosper was doing. She spoke up, her voice high and perhaps a bit quavering. "Don't like that smell," she said, her face screwed up in distaste.

Her mother smoothed back her sweat-tousled hair and said soothingly, "It will help you to feel better faster, sweetheart. You won't smell it at all if you eat a bit of stew now."

Prosper turned away so that Tace wouldn't see the smile that formed on his face at his wife's white lie to the child. Even if the stew might mask the smell of the herb for a moment, there was no way to conceal the bitterness that its aroma promised in its flavor.

As though reading his mind, Kristine said, "If you add some honey to it, the tea will make a sweet for my little sweetheart. Would you like that, Tace?"

The child nodded, though Prosper could see the skepticism — well-founded, he thought — in her expression. He suspected that the best that she could hope for was that it would be at least palatable.

Such was Kristine's power of suggestion, though, that within another hour, the little girl was dosed with the draught, and slept quietly on a pallet beside the hearth while her parents ate their supper in silence.

Chapter 3

"**M**ind that you rake the manure into the soil thoroughly, Cato, and keep an eye on the others to be sure that they do likewise."

The most trustworthy of the field hands nodded in understanding, and for the first time, Prosper noticed that the other man had a few silvery-white hairs among the dark, close-cropped curls atop his head. He sighed inwardly, reflecting that the slave's advancing years meant that he'd need to start saving for a replacement.

Not that he'd have to incur the expense of an experienced hand — Primus would probably do, whenever Cato's time came — but even a likely boy was more money than he wanted to have to spend in these uncertain and troubled times.

Right now, though, Cato was moving off to direct the rest of the field hands to do as Prosper had instructed him. Unless some mishap befell him, the man would be good for another season or two, so the problem of replacing him was one for a later day.

After the previous day's rains, today had dawned clear and warm, and though that meant that the smell of the manure was, if anything, even more overwhelming as a result, it also left the soil just dry enough to plow.

A weary-looking horse — optimistically named Zephyr — pulled the plow at the other end of the field, guided by one of the younger field hands. Another man directed the plow through the field. Both horse and slaves looked as though they longed for the return of the previous day's rain and the enforced leisure it brought.

In another day or two, Prosper knew from experience, both men and beast would become accustomed to this new routine, and their attitudes would improve accordingly, but for the moment, he observed them closely to ensure that they didn't find ways to slack off. However, from what he could see, the rows they plowed were straight and regular, and spaced properly to maximize the crop to come.

Unlike most of the neighboring farms and plantations, Prosper had long felt that corn was a more wholesome and profitable crop to raise than was tobacco. While one could readily survive without a cheroot's noxious smoke billowing from their noses to foul the air all around, corn was a ready source of nutrition, regardless of disruptions to the trade. And, of course, one could always convert it into whiskey, which was both a comfort and a ready item of commerce.

He knew many who found their evenings rendered more serene with a cup of whiskey and a cloud of tobacco smoke to settle their dinner before bedtime, but he wanted no part in the tobacco trade. Prosper thought that the habit of taking smoke left its practitioners' breath foul, their teeth stained, and their wits dulled, until they could again secure their favorite vice.

He'd considered wheat, as bread was a reliable means to satisfy an empty belly, nourished all ages, and helped to set off any kind of a rich meal with a familiar and comforting item. Wheat could also be put to other purposes, of course — biscuit for long travel, the coffin for a high-sided pie, and so on, but corn had a shorter growing season, so it was less sensitive to the vagaries of weather.

Now, of course, he had trained his hands in the planting and tending of corn, too, so it would be difficult to shift to some other crop. Prosper had heard that there were men down in Virginia who were planting corn and wheat together on the same fields and claiming that the combination was beneficial to both crops, but he was skeptical.

The idea of trying to tend to the needs of two different crops as they competed for the same water and soil struck him as risky, and with a house full of children depending upon him, excessive risk was not something that he could accept.

Thinking of the children brought a smile to his face today, unlike the usual sense of unease and worry that they usually brought him. Tace had awoken that morning with her fever having broken in the night and was all smiles as she bounced up from her pallet by the fire.

Her merry giggle had been a relief to both Prosper and Kristine after the uncharacteristic solemness of the prior evening. By the time that Prosper had left to go supervise the plowing, Kristine was keeping a watchful eye on Tace, as the child was closely observing the kittens that their cat had delivered during her illness.

Just at the point of opening their eyes, the tiny creatures were barely more than mewling balls of fur, but they entranced Tace. Soon enough, Prosper knew, they would be running around the house, making trouble, and — he foresaw with certainty — teaching the child the value of respecting their needle-sharp claws.

But for now, they were a source of pure delight, and the

sound of giggles and enthusiastic suggestions for names had followed Prosper out through the door. Prosper didn't know whether the feverfew he'd gotten from Missus Grant had made the difference or not, but he was relieved nonetheless at her recovery.

Almost without conscious intent, his eyes flicked over to the small copse of trees at the far end of the field, under which there were three small stones marking where he and Kristine had laid to rest children who hadn't been able to recover from illnesses that had started much as Tace's had.

The smile on his lips disappeared, replaced with a grim, tight expression. He was glad enough to not be spending the day with a shovel again and tried to dispel the thought from his mind with a jerky shake of his head.

Just then, there was a commotion behind him, and he turned to find that the horse and its guide were at a standstill, and Cato was barking questions at the miserable-looking field hand who stood at the handles of the plow itself. Sighing heavily, Prosper made his way across the field to where the heavy tool sat motionless at the end of a long furrow.

As he approached, he could see that the iron coulter had broken off from the wooden beam of the plow. The stout bolts that held the metal cutting edge of the coulter firmly in place so that it could perform the initial slice through the top layers of the soil had torn right out of the beam. Squatting onto his haunches to examine the splintered sockets where the bolts had been, Prosper shook his head resignedly.

Cato had stopped haranguing the plow driver and now watched as Prosper completed his assessment.

Quietly, he said, "Cato, you may send these men to put

Zephyr in harness for the wagon. We'll need to bring this over to Mister Stone to have a replacement beam fitted."

He glanced over the part of the field that had been plowed — perhaps as much as a quarter of it — and pursed his lips. "If we can get the plow back before the Sabbath, we might yet get this field planted before the season is too far advanced."

Prosper turned to the plow driver. "Jack, you should have been more attentive to how much it was taking to force the plow through such a hard piece of ground. You've set back the planting and cost me a pretty penny in the bargain."

He motioned to Cato. "I'll leave it to you, Cato, to find some suitable task to keep Jack occupied while we wait for the replacement of the plow's beam." He fixed Jack with a sour look and suggested, "Something to remind him to better attend to his duties in the future."

"Yes, sir," both men replied, and Prosper turned away to walk back to the house. He needed to retrieve his purse and be better dressed before he could think of going to deal with Stone.

Not that he disliked the man — far from it — but he wasn't about to present himself at Stone's door in the slops that he'd worn out for what he'd expected was going to be a day of hard, dirty work.

Inside, he busied himself with changing, explaining briefly to Kristine where things stood. "I shall have to draw upon our savings, wife. I had hoped to put the money to some better use, but without we get the plow repaired, there will be no harvest to replenish our larder, never mind any savings to concern ourselves with."

Kristine said nothing, only nodding to acknowledge that

she'd heard him. She was cutting up onions to add to a broth that was simmering over the fire, which he supposed explained why her eyes were bright with what appeared to be unshed tears.

For his own part, the sharp sting of the onions was even reaching him on the other side of the room, as he stood on the tips of his toes to retrieve the heavy crock that held the surplus that he had set aside for a rainy day. Well, yesterday had delivered the rain, and today, the need for the funds.

After selecting what he thought he might need, he added a little more to his hand and dropped the coins into his purse. Returning the crock, lest small hands think it full of mere toys, he nodded curtly to Kristine and went back outside.

There, Cato had not only hitched the horse up to the wagon and loaded the broken plow into the bed but was also busying himself with unfastening all the other parts of the plow from the beam, so that they could deliver up just the broken part for replacement.

Prosper joined him at the task, grunting with the effort of loosening bolts and separating parts that had been joined together for years. When they finished, the gracefully curved piece of oak was now merely heavy, rather than heavy and awkward to maneuver.

Prosper climbed into the seat of the wagon and waited until Cato had jumped into the bed and settled himself before taking up the reins and directing Zephyr back toward the barn. There, he and Cato unloaded and stored the parts they'd removed from the beam, with no more than three words passing between them as they worked.

Back in the wagon, they rode in companionable silence,

each alone with his own thoughts as Zephyr plodded along. The woodworker's shop soon came into view, and after he pulled the wagon to a stop, Prosper jumped down from the seat, motioning with his chin for Cato to bring the damaged beam with him.

He approached the door of Stone's shop and rapped on it with his knuckles. The man answered almost immediately, shavings in his sparse hair, and a curved tool with a wicked-looking keen blade gripped in his hand.

"Oh, it's you, Mister Creale. What brings you to my establishment on this fine day?"

Prosper inclined his head in a respectful greeting, and answered, "One of my field hands has contrived to wreck the beam of my only plow, and I should like very much to get a replacement as quickly as possible. My planting season depends upon it."

Stone pursed his mouth thoughtfully. "Aye, I can see that it would. Ah, this must be the article itself," he said, acknowledging Cato and the heavy wooden component the man carried over his shoulder. Cato shifted it down to carry it with both hands at his waist, so that he could pass through the door, and Stone held out his own hands to accept it from the slave.

He tut-tutted as he inspected the destroyed sockets in the beam, and shook his head, a sour expression on his face. "I wish I could tell you that we could but add bracing on either side and that it would hold up, but plowing applies so much force at this point that it really must consist of sound wood throughout."

Narrowing his eyes in thought for a moment, he said, "I'll tell you what, though. I think I may have a board of ash that will serve. Let me fetch it from my barn, and we shall see whether I can shape it to suit your purpose."

Prosper nodded in grim acceptance, and his gaze followed the man out through the door. He commented to Cato in a low voice, "Ash will be very fine for the purpose, but it will cost a pretty penny — and will take time to shape." Cato said nothing but seemed to be lost in contemplation of the ruined beam.

The woodworker came back, whistling to himself as he maneuvered the stout board on his shoulder through the doorway. He set it down on his workbench and then fetched the damaged part to lay it atop the lumber for the replacement.

"There, you can see that I can easily get a replacement out of this board. My piece is perhaps a little stouter than the original, which will make it both a little heavier and more durable." He smiled encouragingly at Prosper.

For his part, the farmer asked the questions whose answers he was dreading. "How long will it take to form the new beam — and how much will it cost me?"

"Well, it would be best to shape the beam from a piece of green hickory, instead of ash, and then let it cure for a season or longer, before putting it into service. That would be what we'd do if we were building a new plow."

Looking to Prosper for his acknowledgment, he continued as soon as the farmer nodded to him. "Since we need to match the shape of the old beam as closely as possible, though, and we're starting with a board that's already dry, it should do to rough the shape in by saw, and then shave it down to get the details right."

Seeming to sense Prosper's growing impatience, he said, "All together, if I can get some help from Tommy, it shouldn't take but a week or so, what with the other projects I already have in the shop. Now mind you, this is a temporary expedient, because the ash wood will tend to splinter over time, and will warp more easily under normal conditions of usage for a plow than will other kinds of wood."

He pursed his mouth for a moment, considering. "Since this will just get your hands back into the field for this season, what I'd really like to see you do is get a proper hickory replacement started for the long term. If that is acceptable to you, I can do both beams for one price."

"And that price will be . . . ?" Prosper didn't bother to keep his frustration out of his voice. He'd known that Mister Stone would want to do the job the proper way, but he'd also known that the right solution was going to be an expensive one.

The woodworker named a figure, which came to only a bit more than Prosper had expected. He took a deep breath and let it out in a gusty sigh, saying, "That's fair, and I must have the thing, so let's go ahead."

Stone nodded and smiled. "Always a pleasure doing business with you, Mister Creale."

Prosper returned his smile, mechanically, and dug his purse out of his waistcoat.

The other man held up a hand to forestall him. "Nay, nay, you may pay me the first half when I deliver to you the beam of ash, and the second half later this year, when the hickory one is complete."

Prosper nodded and tucked his purse back away. He was turning to leave when the woodworker said, suddenly, "Say, didn't you attend that last sermon that the Methodist fellow, Freeborn Garrettson, delivered in these parts?"

The farmer turned back to face the woodworker. "Aye,

that I did. I found it most interesting and nourishing to my soul."

"Ah, then, you might be interested to hear that he is gathering a group this very evening in my barn, that he may share a fresh account of his salvation with those who are interested."

"Ah, I am most obliged to you for telling me of this, as I am always happy to hear him preach the Gospel. At what hour should I present myself?"

"We expect him to arrive just after supper-time, so that the commands of the flesh do not distract anyone from the word of God."

"A most sensible instruction that is," Prosper said. "I will be here at the appointed time."

Chapter 4

Although the afternoon had turned brisk again, the barn was quite warm, almost stuffy. An excited crowd stood before a makeshift pulpit that Mister Stone had evidently fashioned for the purpose. The woodworker had moved his stock of lumber to line the walls of the barn, leaving plenty of space for what Prosper thought might be more than a score of men.

There was little conversation among the gathered men, who stood and waited in patience. Prosper was pleased to see how many of them he knew from the village and its surrounding community.

Before long, Mister Stone entered the barn, with Mister Garrettson at his side. The preacher followed his host to the front of the room and stepped up to the pulpit, beginning to speak without fanfare.

"My friends," he said, his voice full of emotion. "I am so grateful to be graced with your presence this afternoon, and to share with you my personal experience of the moment that I submitted myself to the mercy of our savior. I hope for each of you that you are moved to seek salvation by hearing my testimony."

He looked out over the crowd, seeming to take the time to meet each man's eyes individually before he began. When his gaze met Prosper's, the farmer felt a shock of recognition in his heart. Here was a man who had heard the voice of God, and Prosper could not help but feel that he was a kindred spirit. However, he did not have long to muse upon this sensation, though, because the preacher began.

"On my way home from an event not so different from this afternoon's, where I listened to Mr. Daniel Ruff preach, just as you are listening to me preach today, I was feeling so oppressed by my ongoing struggle with the enemy of my soul that I was obliged to stop in a forest and alight from my horse."

He closed his eyes, apparently recalling the pain of his struggle. "I bowed on my knees before the Lord, and immediately felt the sensation of two spirits striving within me. The good Spirit set forth to my mind the beauties of religion, and I felt almost ready to lay hold upon my Savior."

"But oh, unbelief, soul-damning sin — it kept me in that moment from my Jesus. And then the enemy arose on the other hand and dressed religion in as odious a garb as possible. He seemed for a moment to set the world and the things of it in the most brilliant colors before me and told me that all these things should be mine if I would but give up my false notions and serve him."

The preacher shook his head at the memory, and continued, "His temptations, I must confess to you now, might be compared to a sweeping rain, and they consumed me as the storm consumes a field."

Prosper knew all too well what that was like, and he felt himself frowning at the imagery.

"I continued on my knees for a considerable time, and at last I began to give way to the reasoning of the enemy. My tender feelings toward my Savior abated, and my tears were gone. My heart was hardened, but I remained on my knees in a kind of meditation. At length, I addressed my Maker thus: 'Lord, spare me one year more, and by that time I can put my worldly affairs in such a train that I can serve thee.'"

Mister Garrettson closed his eyes and shook his head mournfully. "Again, I had the clear sensation of the two spirits there with me, present in that forest. The answer came to me, as clearly as though it had been spoken aloud, 'Now is the accepted time.'"

His voice rose, and he said, "I then pleaded for six months, but was denied — one month, no! — I then asked for just one week, and again the answer came, 'This is the time.'"

He took a deep breath and held it, his eyes again closed as he remembered the moment. He opened them and continued, looking out over the heads of the crowd as though at some specter in the distance. "For some time, the devil was silent, till I was denied even one week in his service, and then it was he who shot a powerful dart. 'The God,' said he, 'you are attempting to serve is a hard Master, and I would have you desist from your endeavor.'"

Mister Garrettson's gaze returned to the men gathered before him, and he said in an almost conversational tone, "Carnal people know very little of this kind of exercise, but it was as perceptible to me as if I had been conversing with two people, face to face. As soon as this argument's powerful temptation came, I felt my heart rise — I do not say with enmity — against my Maker, and I immediately arose from my knees, saying, 'I will take my own time, and then I will serve Thee.'"

Clenching his teeth as though shocked by his own past actions, he said, "I mounted my horse with a hard unbelieving heart, unwilling to submit to Jesus. Oh, what a good God I had to deal with! I might in justice have been sent to hell in that very moment."

Prosper felt a flush of heat in his ears. What God-fearing man had not harbored the same thought when he had acted according to his own desires — placed there by the devil, no doubt — instead of following the commands of the Lord? His attention was drawn back to the preacher when he picked up his narrative after pausing to collect himself from this awful memory.

"I had not ridden a quarter of a mile before the Lord met me powerfully with these words: 'These three years have I come seeking fruit on this fig tree and find none.' Before I had time to ponder His meaning, He added, 'I have come once more to offer you life and salvation, and it is the last time: choose or refuse.'"

He voiced God's word in a tone both somber and full of menace. Now, his voice conveyed wonder and astonishment as he continued. "I was instantly surrounded by a divine power: heaven and hell were disclosed to my view, and life and death were set before me."

Mister Garrettson's gaze again sought the eyes of individuals among the men listening raptly before him. Quietly, he said, "I do believe that if I had rejected this call, mercy would have been forever taken from me. I knew the very instant when I submitted to the Lord and was willing that Christ should reign over me. I likewise knew the two sins which I parted with last: pride, and unbelief."

Shaking himself as though emerging from a dream, he concluded, "Well, I threw the reins of my bridle onto my horse's neck, put my hands together, and cried out, 'Lord, I submit!' I was less than nothing in my own sight, and was now, for the first time, reconciled to the justice of God. The enmity my heart was slain, the path of salvation was open to me, and I saw a beauty in the perfections of the Deity and felt that power of faith and love that I had been a stranger to before."

He bowed his head, his eyes closed as though in silent prayer, and then raised his head again, nearly shouting now. "Do you feel that power within your hearts, gentlemen? Or is the enemy still at work in your mind, tempting you to serve his purposes for just another year, just another six months, a month, a week, an hour? Have you laid down your life before the Lord completely, or are you still carrying the burden of your sins upon your own back?"

He stepped down from the pulpit now and moved into the crowd, challenging individual members of the gathering. Stopping before Eleazar Ball, whose hands were clasped before his rheumy eyes in the attitude of fervent prayer, the preacher took his hands and asked, "Brother, have you accepted Christ to reign over your life?" Eleazar nodded briskly, apparently beyond the capacity for speech.

Prosper harbored doubts about the full sincerity of Eleazar's commitment to God, given that he could almost smell the alehouse vapors from across the room, but Mister Garrettson seemed satisfied, and moved on to the next man.

"And you," he said to Thomas Fitchburg, a hard-faced merchant, who stood with his arms crossed over his chest, a half-frown on his lips. "Are you ready to welcome the Lamb of God into your heart?"

Fitchburg spoke quietly and firmly, but with no malice in his tone. "Not at this time, brother, for I am still too attached to my sins to give them up to another." He motioned with his chin for the preacher to move on to his next subject, but Mister Garrettson paused still for a moment, a thoughtful expression in his eyes.

"I shall pray for you, brother, and for your release from the enemy's snares."

Fitchburg acknowledged this with a taciturn nod, and Mister Garrettson continued to move through the crowd, spending time with each man in turn. When he reached Prosper, the farmer smiled and shook his head.

"I am already committed to the Lord, brother. Give your attention to someone who needs it more."

The preacher returned his smile and took Prosper's hands, holding them up to examine them. "Your fingers tell a story of commitment to the earth, my friend, but this is a matter between you and God, and nothing that you need convince me of. I will ask only that you listen to the voice of your Lord, when he speaks to you."

Mister Garrettson released his hands and turned away to the next man before Prosper had registered what he'd said. Had the preacher somehow sensed that he'd heard an unexpected voice just the day prior? Was this proof that God was not only speaking to him, but was advising the preacher as to the state of his soul?

Prosper was glad enough to escape into the night, having dropped a couple of coins into the hat that Mister Stone passed around for Mister Garrettson's benefit, as the gathering broke up. The stars shone through the still-naked tree branches as he hurried along the road home, eager for the warmth of his home and hearth.

Mister Garrettson's testimony tonight gave him much to ponder as he walked. As a practical matter, could he now anticipate having not one, but two voices address him at various times, as God and the devil each strove to win him over to their side? Prosper had meant what he'd said to Mister Garrettson — he was quite certain of his commitment to the service of God — but if that were so, then why would either spirit seek to speak to him?

If, as the voice had advised him, much was required of him, what might that mean? Would God command him to take up the life that Mister Garrettson pursued, sharing the Gospel as an itinerant preacher, traveling far from home? Or would his service to God be something more mundane, such as Mister Stone's support of the preacher and opening his barn for use as a meeting-house?

For that matter, a barn was hardly a proper meeting place for a congregation that grew larger every time that Mister Garrettson came through the community. Perhaps it was time to consider building a proper chapel, an effort that would require both manpower and money. Mister Garrettson had mentioned that he'd done likewise in his own community, and it was possible that this comment was a means for the spirit to plant the idea in other minds further afield.

In any event, it seemed likely that Prosper's routine was on the edge of being overturned, and the thought sent a shiver down his spine that had nothing to do with the chill in the air.

Chapter 5

The new ash-wood beam was holding up to Prosper's satisfaction, although it didn't have quite the same shape as the original oaken one. He and Cato had particularly struggled to get the handles fixed in the same position as they had been before.

As a result, Jack had been forced to hold the handles at an awkward angle as he drove the plow on the first day after they'd reassembled the tool.

The slave was now prostrate on his litter, his face a rictus of pain.

"Can't even hardly stand up, sir," he said to Prosper, who had come in answer to Cato's summons. Prosper felt equal parts of concern for the man, and frustration that his carelessness with the plow had led to this circumstance in the first place.

Glancing up from where he had crouched to examine the suffering man, Prosper found Cato's anxious face. "Has Miss Annie been called?" Mister Wrangell's slave often came to minister to the health of Prosper's hands, as he had no slaves with her depth of experience in their care.

"Not yet, sir," Cato answered. "I wanted to give you a chance to speak to Jack first."

Prosper nodded and stood. "Well, let's get her here and have her get a poultice on this fellow's back. Can Peter take over driving the plow today?" Peter was not Prosper's first choice for the job, being a young man with veering ideas about responsibility, but with Jack unable for the time being to do the work, he had to have someone.

Cato said immediately, "Yes, sir," then added, "I will want to lead Zephyr, to keep an eye on Peter, however. He has driven it before, but not for a spring plowing. Takes a bit more attention, as you know."

Prosper agreed, "Aye, I know." Turning back to the litter, he said, "Jack, Miss Annie will have you back at work in no time, don't you worry. In the meantime, you take it easy and rest today."

Jack didn't answer, but only groaned and turned on his litter to find a more comfortable position. Leading Cato through the door of the slave quarters back into the daylight, Prosper said, "Let's you and I go and see if we can't get those handles right, so that this doesn't happen again. Peter's of a size with Jack, isn't he?"

"Little taller," Cato said, "But he should be close enough that neither he nor Jack gets crippled up again."

"Very well," Prosper said. "You fetch Peter, and I'll get the tools and get started." He sighed in frustration as he made his way back to the barn where Jack and Cato had dragged the plow, its new beam bright and clean against the contrast with the older components.

The point at which the handle attached to the beam was nowhere near as rugged as where the coulter and main plow blade's attached. Most of the power being delivered from the horse's harness needed to go into the ground through those heavy connections, while the handle only needed to carry the plow driver's steering to direct the plow's path through the ground.

As a result, there were just two stout pegs forming the attachment, and Prosper busied himself with loosening those while he waited for Cato and Peter. As he worked, he was thinking through how to adjust the angle at which the handle stood when the plow was in its working attitude.

The top peg was showing signs of loosening when the unwelcome miracle — for Prosper had become convinced that it was a miracle, but did not understand why he had been so blessed — happened again.

"Much is required of you, but the way will soon be revealed."

Prosper froze. Had he actually heard a voice again, or had it merely been his ears ringing with the echo of the hammer against the peg? He had nearly convinced himself that this was the case when the voice sounded once more, in a tone that was almost reassuring.

"It will not be long now."

This time, there was no mistaking it. The voice was the same as the one he had heard in the field, and it had again been as plain as if someone were standing right behind him. The barn was empty aside from him, though — Cato must be having trouble tracking down Peter — so there was again no chance that it was merely a prank.

He closed his eyes and sighed, permitting himself to wonder why God had chosen to reveal Himself to a humble farmer. He remembered then that Mister Garrettson had been little more than the same when God had set that worthy man upon his path.

Prosper did not feel worthy, nor could he imagine that there was anything he could do that was so valuable to God that He might choose to use him as the means of accomplishing it, but at least He had said that the 'way would soon be revealed.' If he was going to be given an arduous task, Prosper would appreciate some clear instructions.

Trying to put God's latest visitation out of his mind, he got the first peg loose and had started in on the second when Cato appeared, with a chastened-looking Peter trailing behind him.

Prosper said nothing about their delayed appearance, but Cato explained, "He traded tasks with old Frankie, and then with Big George, and I found him taking his ease while he made the new boy do his work."

Peter said nothing in his own defense, but looked away, shame painted across his features. Prosper gave the young man a disapproving shake of his head and turned back to his work. He thought that the slave's ear looked as though it was already swelling from the boxing that Cato must have delivered to it, and there seemed little use in adding to the punishment that Cato had thought appropriate.

"I've got the one peg out, and this one's loose enough to make the adjustment. Peter, I'll have you take up the handle and hold it just as though you were driving the plow."

Peter sheepishly moved from behind Cato, where he'd almost been hiding from what he imagined Prosper's wrath might be, and took up the handles as directed. Prosper looked at the position of the peg holes on the beam and on the handle and grunted to himself.

"Looks as though Mister Stone missed the mark by just a bit when he tried to give me a copy of the old beam, but with a little chisel work and a shim or two, we should be able to get it right.

Hold it steady if you would, Peter."

He busied himself with the tools, the hard ash wood of the beam requiring more force than he was accustomed to applying. He abandoned the effort to simply twist the chisel against the sides of the peg hole as futile. Next, he tried striking the end of the chisel's handle, but the plow jumped away and the chisel only left a dent beside the hole.

He called out, "Cato, would you come and brace this beam, so that I can direct the chisel against a fixed target?" He knew that the right way to do the job would be to completely disassemble the plow and work the beam on a bench or the ground, but he was impatient to get the device back into service.

Cato moved into position, and Prosper cautioned him, "Mind that you stay far enough back from where I'm working that the chisel won't strike you as it comes through the other side, now."

Cato nodded. "Yes, sir. I've got it." He gripped the beam above his bent knee, applying force downward to pin the wood into place, and Prosper was satisfied that it was secure enough to work on.

Afterward, Prosper was never quite sure what went wrong. He placed the chisel where he needed to make the cut and struck it solidly with his hammer to drive it through the beam to enlarge the peg hole.

Somehow, the point of the chisel jumped from where he'd intended to cut, and skittered over the top of the beam instead, lodging deep in Cato's thigh.

The slave uttered a hoarse shout and fell away, clutching at the handle of the chisel. The force of Prosper's blow had driven the keenly-honed tip of the tool into Cato's leg right up to the handle, and as the man dropped to the ground, Prosper could already see the shockingly crimson stain blooming outward to cover the leg of his trousers.

Cato struggled to prop himself up on his elbows, his legs splayed out under the beam of the plow, and he looked dumbly at the handle protruding from his leg, and at the blood that flowed freely from under it, soaking into the packed earth of the barn floor. The sharp, coppery tang of its odor rose at once to Prosper's nose, striking fear into his heart.

Both Prosper and Peter were immediately by the stricken man's side, but the pool of blood that spread out around the groaning slave made it clear to Prosper that this was a mortal wound. Peter looked frantically from Cato's face to Prosper's, but neither of them answered the desperate question on his face.

Prosper looked Cato in the eyes, and said to him, emotion choking his voice, "I am sorry, Cato."

Cato's expression held surprise, and he replied, "Mister Creale, what has happened to me? I feel so . . . "

They never learned what Cato felt, because his eyes rolled up into the back of his head, and he collapsed, completely limp.

Chapter 6

Prosper sighed heavily, closing the door behind himself. He had finished supervising Peter, Jacob and Cain in laying Cato to rest, and he'd had Peter send Primus to talk with him.

The man was substantially taller than Prosper was, and he'd always felt uncomfortable with how he had to crane his head back when giving him his tasks for the day. Although he hadn't planned it, he was glad enough that he had already seated himself on a bench outside of the barn when Primus arrived.

"Sit, Primus, for we must talk."

The slave sat, saying, "I done heard what happened to Mister Cato, and I'm surely sorrowed at the news."

"I am sorry to have to share it, too. He was one of the few hands I could trust to keep the rest in line and working on what needs doing. I need you to take over in his place, and the job is going to be twice as hard with so many of the hands mourning for Cato."

"Yes, sir. Cato was a good man, and we all done respected him. I don't know if they'll respect me as well."

Prosper chewed his lip and shook his head, then answered. "They've just got to, or else we'll not get the crop in the ground in time to harvest this year."

Primus said nothing but looked at the ground miserably.

"You see that, don't you, Primus?"

"Yes, sir, I do. Can I speak my mind plainly, sir?"

Prosper nodded.

"I know that you and Missus Creale have got to attend to the good of the whole plantation. If there is no crop, you can't afford to keep us, and there ain't none of us want to be sold someplace else."

"I've no plans to sell any of you off, except maybe a couple who don't do their work. I need every one of you to do your part, it is true."

Primus set his mouth in a grim line, but he said nothing.

After a long silence, Prosper said, "If you can get the field plowed and the seed in the ground before the week is out, I won't even need to consider that much." He didn't add that he thought that he'd probably be better off trading some of the less motivated hands for another good, reliable man. Still, if Primus could get the hands to do what was needed, he could leave them all in place, he supposed.

Primus looked out over the half-plowed field, the first furrows of which were already sprouting the crop that they had been able to get into them after the plow had broken. His mouth sank into a deep frown of thought as he looked from one end to the other of the open space.

Finally, he said, "I will see what we can do, sir. I cannot make you no promises, but I will see what we can do."

Prosper had dismissed Primus and had wearily turned back to the tedious work of properly dismantling the plow. He still had to complete the needed adjustments to the peg hole. With the beam now sitting bare, he held it tight to the bench by the lever clamp, while he finished the work with the chisel.

He tried to ignore the stains on the chisel's handle and resolved to have a new handle made as soon as possible. He reassembled the plow and satisfied himself that it was good enough before going back into the house.

Now, as he shed his boots at the door, he noted with a grimace that they too bore dark stains where Cato's blood had splashed them. He sighed heavily at the unpleasant task to come. Entering the kitchen, he saw that Tace and little Phillip were playing together in the corner as his wife worked some sort of dough at the table.

He said gruffly, "Children, I need you to go upstairs for a little while. I need to speak to your mother in confidence."

Tace said nothing, but rose and took Phillip by the hand, leading him out of the kitchen. Something about Prosper's tone brooked no argument, and he was grateful to avoid a scene before the upset to come.

When he heard the sounds of their light feet moving across the floor upstairs, he turned to his wife, who had stopped working the dough and was looking at him with an expression of concern. He said without preamble, "Cato's dead. There was an accident, and he was gone before we could so much as attempt to bind his wound."

Kristine's hands flew to her mouth, her eyes wide with shock. "Oh, that is awful news, husband," she said. "I hope he did not suffer?"

"I do not think that he did, no. As I said, it was quick. I've asked Primus to take over the management of the hands in his stead."

She nodded, clearly not yet focused on the practical matters of running the plantation without Cato's knowledge and the relative respect that he had commanded among the hands.

"Have you told his woman?"

Prosper looked sharply at Kristine. "What woman?"

"Why, I thought you had given him your blessing to go and pass time with her each Sabbath eve."

Prosper's eyebrows drew together. "I gave him leave to visit Wrangell's place after all his work was done at the end of the week, but I had no conception that he had a woman over there. The old rascal never elaborated on the nature of his 'friends' there."

Kristine shook her head, her mouth pulled into an exasperated look. "I heard him and Primus talking about her, and I confess that I was a little taken aback that you had permitted him the liberty, but I did not want to interfere with your management of the hands."

Prosper could not argue the point, but said only, "Well, in any event, no, I did not tell his woman, as I do not even know who she might be." Thoughtfully, he added, "As it appears that Primus knew of her, I trust he will inform her in due course."

Then he clapped his hand to his forehead. "I forgot all about that dratted fellow Jack, in the hurry of the moment and then getting Cato into the ground." Seeing Kristine's confusion, he explained, "He hurt himself trying to use the plow without getting the handle properly affixed to the new beam. We'll need all the hands fit to work, if we're to get the crop in before the season is too far advanced."

Kristine nodded but said nothing in reply. He stepped back to the door and opened it, peering out. He called out, "You, there,

Frankie!"

A doleful-looking old slave, whose hair was white against his dark skin, Frankie came hurrying over at his owner's call. "Yes, sir?"

"Go on over to Mister Wrangell's and ask him to send Annie over to tend to Jack and his hurt back. You may tell him that I will pay him the usual fee for her services."

"Yes, sir, I'll fetch Annie over here, and tell Mister Wrangell that you'll settle up with him."

"Just so. And Frankie?"

"Yes, sir?"

"Was Annie old Cato's woman over there?"

"No, sir." The reminder of Cato's death brought a new depth of sadness over the old man's face, but he offered nothing further.

Prosper let the answer lie in the air for a moment before shrugging and waving the old man on his way. Frankie loped off, and Prosper watched him go, his customary scowl deepening for a moment. He closed the door and returned to the kitchen.

"We are surely having a terrible run of luck," he remarked. "Between the plow, and now this, what little I've put aside will soon be exhausted, and there is still no assurance that we'll be able to get a crop this year."

Kristine did not answer him, nor would Prosper have welcomed her comment. He was speaking more to himself than to her, in any event. The problems of the management of the plantation were entirely his own to solve. He sighed and sat heavily on the bench.

He would have liked more time to save and plan for the

inevitable replacement for Cato. To lose him so suddenly was not only a shock to the already disrupted operations of the plantation, but also to the delicate balance of his financial situation. He had to confess to himself, too, that the man had been the nearest thing to a friend that he had among the hands, and even if Primus might prove to be a competent overseer, he seemed unlikely to replace Cato in that regard.

Prosper rubbed the back of his neck, which was stiffening up under the burden of his worries, and pondered his options. He could try to get through this season with just the hands that he already had, and trust that Primus could keep them in order. If the man could even improve their reliability, it was just possible that the profits from the year's crop would enable him to bring on another prime boy, or even a proved man.

However, if they continued to be as unreliable as they had been in the past, he could not be certain that he could keep all of them, even if the crop did go into the ground in time.

Raising corn required constant attention, eliminating pests and clearing out weeds, and inattention or just plain laziness would cause a decreased yield, which would inevitably decrease the profit to be found at harvest.

And all of this was, of course, depending upon the continued remoteness of the conflict between the rebels and the King's troops. That raised a whole set of horrible possibilities that scarcely could bear consideration.

He had heard of battles taking place on farms in Massachusetts and even as close as Virginia, and he shuddered to think of the state of that farmland after the fallen soldiers had been collected and the warring forces had moved on to some other unfortunate ground.

Even just the presence of a peaceful encampment would leave devastation in its wake, to say nothing of the inevitable looting of foodstuffs and supplies to keep any army in fit condition to fight. The papers had been full of lurid stories, and rumors about town had been far worse.

As was his usual practice, Prosper did his best to shake off the gloomy thoughts of what might happen should the war visit their community. He comforted himself with the knowledge that no force had yet been reported anywhere in the colony, nor was there that much of strategic value here.

The self-styled "Continental Congress" was meeting in Philadelphia, which was comfortably far away. Nearer by, the only violence that had broken out so far had been a couple of years prior, when a group of hotheads at Annapolis took it upon themselves to join the protests against the crackdown on tea smuggling.

The burning of an innocent merchant ship for the supposed offense of bringing taxed tea into the harbor at Annapolis had stirred up enough unrest that the trade with the mother country had still not returned to a normal basis.

As a result, the threat of actual war remained at least at arm's length, and so Prosper could convince himself that he need take no immediate measures to guard against it. If fate brought it to his community, there was little he could do about it, anyway.

He shook his head sharply in frustration. His mind wandered so in recent days! The immediate problems still stood before him and needed to be solved. The plow should now be usable, and if Primus could get Peter to work in the morning, the rest of the hands could get the seed into the ground as quickly as

Peter turned the furrows.

After that, he would have to count on good weather and the hands' diligent attention to their duties to see the crop through the rest of the season. He believed that Primus understood the importance of the job ahead of them, but it remained to be seen whether he could do any better than Cato had at keeping the rest of them on task.

The revelation that Cato had kept the secret of his dalliance with one of Wrangell's slaves had shaken Prosper's belief in the reliability of the dead man's management of the hands. He had to consider the possibility that there might have been other secrets, and that he might have misplaced his faith in Cato.

There was nothing to be gained by dwelling on Cato's failings, whatever they might have been, of course. It only underscored the importance of keeping a closer eye on Primus than he had on Cato. The man was not as keen-witted as Cato had been, but it might just be that this would make him less prone to mischief than Cato had apparently been.

Chapter 7

The weather, while far from perfect, had been good enough. Similarly, the hands had done their duty well enough, and the corn seemed to grow almost fast enough to see it move as it stretched from the soil toward the sun.

The hands were attending to their duties well enough, and there were few weeds. Not enough, at least, to choke out the roots of the cornstalks, nor to shade them with spreading leaves.

Mister Wrangell's Annie had gotten Jack back on his feet within a few days, and after he was recovered, the young man had sought Prosper out.

"I can't hardly bear the thought that Cato died because of me," the slave told him, his face twisted up in sadness and remorse. "I surely wish that I had been more careful with the plow."

"What's done is done," Prosper said brusquely. "Haven't you work you ought to be attending to?" He could see the young man's face fall at the dismissal.

Prosper knew that he ought to hear the man out and accept his apology in good grace, but the fact was that he had harbored many a bitter thought about the costs he had borne as a result of Jack's failings.

The financial burden of the repairs to the plow and the eventual need to replace Cato was severe enough. The more subtle disruptions to the running of the plantation, though, were almost worse. Primus was willing enough to take on the expanded role that Prosper had asked of him, but not all the other hands were as happy to accept him in place of Cato.

In particular, Cain, whom Prosper might have considered in Primus' place if he'd been a little more responsible, made it very clear that he thought that he should have been the one to be given the additional responsibilities. While he said nothing directly to Prosper, Cain stirred up trouble among the other hands, and word filtered back to him that some hands thought that the man was in danger of living up to his namesake.

After seeing Primus limping around with a swollen lip, which he confessed had resulted from a fight with Cain, Prosper had had enough. He stormed into the slave quarters and called out, "Cain, you come with me, now."

His tone permitted no argument, and Cain rose from where he'd been resting on his pallet, moving with just enough of a delay to demonstrate a touch of insolence.

Without even thinking, Prosper reached out and cuffed the man across his ear. "You need to move when I call you, and all the more so when you are to answer for your behavior!"

Cain stood and gaped at him in disbelief, and Prosper realized that he had never before struck the man — indeed, he could not remember the last time that he had struck any of his slaves — and that Cain was genuinely shocked at being physically disciplined.

Prosper growled, "I said to come with me," and turned to leave the quarters. He heard Cain stir into motion, shuffling along behind him as they emerged into the springtime sun.

Once outside, Prosper turned back to face the other man.

Putting a finger right under the slave's nose, he said, "There will be no fighting among my hands, under any circumstances. You've gone and crippled up Primus, and I need him fit for work, just as I need all of you."

The defiant light in the slave's eyes still burned, though, and Prosper decided that he needed to try another tactic to get through to the younger man. "I cannot afford to have a hand on my plantation who is going to stir up trouble, get into fights, and defy my will. I've half a mind to sell you off and buy a man I can depend upon in your place."

Cain said nothing, but the muscles of his jaw jumped, as though he was biting back a reply.

Prosper almost wished that he would talk back, as it would make his decision all the easier. He demanded, "Well? What have you to say for yourself?"

Cain said, after a pause, "I don't like taking direction from the Primus. When I heard about poor old Cato, I expected that you would have me take his place, and instead you chose a man who's only been on the plantation for a few years. I done spent near my whole life working for you, and it don't sit right that you make me answer to him."

Prosper said, in an exasperated tone, "It's not for you to judge my decisions about the jobs that I ask anyone on the plantation to perform. Primus has been here long enough for me to have come to an understanding of his qualities. I've despaired of seeing you exhibit those qualities over these many years, Cain."

Cain scowled, but looked down at his feet, saying nothing.

"You are not owed a role of greater responsibility simply due to your years, or how long you've worked for me. It is a thing that is based entirely on your behavior."

Prosper shook his head, his mouth still held in a tight, grim line. He continued, "Starting a fight with Primus is just the sort of thing that demonstrates the very problem I am speaking of. If you truly do hope to improve your station, you must earn that privilege — and the first step is to conduct yourself as though you already had the responsibilities of the role you want to earn."

Cain sighed and lifted his head at last. "Yes, sir," he said quietly. "I did not understand how you see things, but I think I do now."

Prosper threw his hands up. "It is not just a matter of how I see things, but one of how I must run this plantation in order to assure our very survival."

He waved a hand out over the surrounding countryside. "I know that it likely doesn't much reach your ears, but these are uncertain times, with events far beyond any of our control threatening to overwhelm us all. The breaking of a plow and the death of a trusted hand are disasters in good times, but they could be catastrophes now."

Prosper shook his head, grimacing at the absurdity of explaining the complexities of the world to a slave. He concluded sternly, "It comes to this. If we are to have any chance to weather these circumstances, I need everyone to do their jobs, as well as you all know how, without any further nonsense."

"Yes, sir." Cain's eyes held none of their earlier defiance, but there was little more than mute acceptance of the total authority of a master over a slave. Prosper's more detailed explanations had, it seemed, scarcely registered.

Prosper sighed. "Go and do the work in the barn that I

had assigned to Primus, and tell him I said to rest and use some of Annie's poultices to improve his eye. Then, when you have all of that done, you must complete your own work for the day, as well, no matter how long it all takes you."

Cain scowled, but said nothing more than simply, "Yes, sir," before moving off to do as he was told.

Prosper watched the man walk away and snorted to himself. Perhaps what God was giving him in this time was just trouble that he must overcome.

Sighing heavily once again, Prosper made his way back to the house, moving stiffly as he drew off his boots at the door.

Besides having to directly manage too many of the hands, he had had no choice but to undertake some of the work himself this morning, repairing a fence trampled at daybreak by Wrangell's cows.

The fresh shoots of the growing corn had obviously proved irresistible to the dumb beasts, and it had taken Prosper most of the morning to straighten toppled fence posts and to restore the trampled and broken rails. There was no point in demanding that his neighbor perform the repair, because the cows would just be back in Prosper's field the next day.

The work they already had assigned to them occupied his hands' time, leaving only Prosper himself as both trustworthy and available. At least the ground was still soft enough to work with. The soil at the margins of the field was a bit more densely packed than that of the active growing portion, but he was able to get the posts seated and braced with a few spades full of dirt packed tight around them.

The rails had been another matter. The cattle had trampled

and splintered several, and he had to go and find suitable replacements from the fallen trees in the margins of the field. Splitting them had taken more effort, and getting them secured with fresh pegs to the posts had taken him nearly to supper time — with a brief interruption to speak with Cain.

Hearing Prosper's boots fall to the floor, Tace came running in to the front hall from the kitchen. She threw her arms around his leg, nearly knocking him off balance, and said proudly, "Daddy, Mama let me help today!"

Prosper braced himself against the wall and then bent to pick her up. "Did she, now? What did she let you help with?"

"I got to sort rocks and beans," she said.

"Your mama has rocks in the kitchen that she had you sort?"

Tace giggled. "No, silly," she said. "There were rocks in the beans, and she had me take them out."

"That sounds like a very important job," he said seriously. His mood was already lightening under the influence of the child's enthusiasm.

"Yes," said Tace, wriggling to be let down. He set her feet back on the floor, and she took off running, passing out of sight into the kitchen. He could hear her excited voice as she told Kristine what she'd said to him.

Entering the kitchen himself, he could smell the meaty, rich scent of the beans simmering in their pot over the fire. Kristine glanced up from the loaf of bread she was just getting shaped, and said, "Long day?"

He sat heavily on the bench by the hearth, stretching his cold feet toward the fire. "Aye." He knew from experience that she would not attend if he laid out all the details, but appreciated her taking notice that he looked more weary than usual.

Still, in this instance, he decided he wanted to see whether she had any insights, as she had at times in the past been able to point out subtleties in the interactions between the hands that he had not noticed.

He mopped his brow with the sleeve of his shirt and said, "Cain believes that I should have given him the role of being our slave driver, instead of Primus."

Kristine looked up, her eyes cast toward the ceiling as she considered. "Primus has long been Cato's protégé, so it was not at all a surprise to me when you elevated him on Cato's passing. Cain might have been a better choice, had he been under Cato's tutelage, but I suspect Cato passed him over because he is too impetuous, too likely to make decisions based on pure emotion, instead of facts."

She looked down from the ceiling to meet Prosper's eyes. "If you could have asked Cato before he died, I do not think that he would have suggested even considering Cain."

Prosper nodded. "Cain started a fight with Primus this afternoon, and I told him that the mere fact that he had fought with another slave was enough to show that he could not have done the job."

Kristine's eyebrows shot up. "Fighting? Oh, my. Yes, you made the correct choice, and I hope that you have impressed upon Cain the importance of self-control in a man in his position."

"Oh, yes. I did not resort to the lash — though I confess that I was sorely tempted — but I compelled him to add Primus' labors to his own today. He left Primus with an eye swollen shut, and when I am already short-handed, too."

Kristine scowled. "You should probably sell that boy off, just to stop him from causing more trouble here."

"I told him I was of a mind to do just that, but I'd rather wait and see whether the instruction I offered him today has sunk in, and whether he can improve his behavior and attitude. Trying to incorporate a new hand into the plantation right now would take more time and energy than I have to spare."

She nodded. "I can see the reason in that. Still, if he goes around injuring the other hands, we are better off without him, and you should not hesitate to send him off."

He only grunted in reply, signifying that he was through discussing the issue, but he was glad that her perception of the matter supported his own.

"Oh," she said, "Before I forget, Mister Stone sent a note for you." Calling out to their daughter, she said, "Tace, can you please get the paper on the little table in the front hall?"

The girl jumped up from the floor where she'd been playing with a handful of pebbles — doubtless the rocks sorted out from the beans — and ran out to the hallway. Returning, she handed her father the note, saying breathlessly, "Here you go, Papa."

He kissed the top of her head, and she smiled joyfully at him, then returned to her play. He turned the paper over, and opened it, reading.

"Mister Garrettson is returning to preach the Gospel this very evening, and Mister Stone knows how much I enjoy that man's words. I shall need to clean myself up and change into suitable clothing after supper."

Kristine said only, "You have time to get washed while the bread bakes, if you like."

He smiled at her fondly, glad that she understood the importance of such meetings, and rose from the bench, his energy restored.

"I do believe that I shall do just that, my dear friend. I am most excited to hear what Mister Garrettson has to say this time."

Chapter 8

The preacher started in without preliminaries when he stepped up to the pulpit. "For the good of others, I should like to speak of a few days of the exercise I have undergone of late in my struggles against our great foe, and the startling conclusions I have drawn from those experiences." Mister Garrettson's face looked drawn and haggard in comparison with his former appearance, and Prosper was frankly worried for the man's health.

However, he dismissed these thoughts to listen raptly as the preacher continued. "The blessed Redeemer left me, or rather hid his face from me, and I had to wade through deep waters of doubt on my own. I fasted and prayed until I was almost reduced to a skeleton but did not open my mouth to any living being."

He drank thirstily from the cup of water on the makeshift pulpit, and a boy hurried to refill it while he went on. "I was sinking into desperation. Oh, how powerfully I was harassed by the devil, day and night! That following Saturday, I was walking through the fields. All of nature was clothed with beauty and verdure, but I could discover no charms in aught around me."

"I was under the deepest exercises of the mind, and severely tempted by the Devil. 'Ah,' suggested he, 'where is your God now?' He thrust atheism and deism at me, and suggested to my mind, 'You see you have been deluded, and if you now take my advice, you will deny every pretension to this religion.' The enemy said to me, 'The Methodists are a set of enthusiasts, and you have now a proof of this.'"

Mister Garrettson glared angrily about the room, and Prosper had to remind himself that the preacher was angry at Satan, and not the members of this congregation. He waited for Mister Garrettson to elaborate on what proof Satan had presented him with, but the preacher rolled onward without filling in the details.

"Then, he exhibited to my imagination all of the splendors of the world by way of temptation, and said to me, 'All these things will I give to you if you will deny that God you have been attempting to serve and pray to him no more.' I was sunk as low as I could possibly be, for my mind was encompassed with darkness and the most severe distress."

Prosper could see that Mister Garrettson's eyes were welling up with tears at the painful memory. "I was afraid that my lips would be forced open to deny the God who made me. Glory, glory to my Lord, who at that moment again gave me a view of an opening eternity, and a sense of his dread majesty, the sight of which brought me into the dust, prostrate with my face to the ground."

A tear trickled down the preacher's face, and Prosper could not help but feel his own eyes starting to flow in sympathetic emotion. Mister Garrettson continued, "I lay there for a considerable time with the thought in my mind, 'Oh, Lord, if I perish now, it shall be at Thy feet, crying for Thy mercy.' Thus I lay till I recovered a glimmer of hope that I should be saved at last."

He drank again and wiped his eyes. "I arose from the earth

at last, and advancing toward the house in deep thought, I came to this conclusion: That I would exclude myself from the society of men and live in a cell upon no more than bread and water, mourning out my days for having aggrieved my Lord."

The depth of the man's belief filled Prosper with admiration, and he saw the man's evident sorrow for having moments of doubt, when faced with a determined foe that would have defeated any man lacking such faith.

"I went into my room and sat in one position until the hour of nine o'clock. I then threw myself onto the bed and slept until morning. Although the next day was the Lord's day, I did not intend to go to any place of worship. Neither did I desire to see any person, but wished to pass my time away in total solitude."

He seemed to shrink into himself even in just the retelling of the story, but he steadied and went on. "I continued reading the Bible till eight, and then, under a sense of duty, called my family together for prayer. As I stood with a book in my hand, in the act of giving out a hymn, a thought struck powerfully in my mind."

He stood straighter and said, "I knew it to be the same blessed Voice which had spoken to me before, and it said to me, 'It is not right for you to keep your fellow-creatures in bondage. You must let the oppressed go free.'"

A murmur passed through the crowd, but Mister Garrettson seemed to take no note of the effect his revelation was having upon his audience. "Until that moment, I had never suspected that the practice of slave-keeping was wrong. I had not read any book on the subject, nor engaged in any arguments with my fellow slave-keepers. I paused but a minute, and then replied, 'Lord, the oppressed will go free.'"

The stirring in the crowd became more audible now, but still Garrettson ignored it. "I was in that moment as clear of them in my mind as if I had never owned one. I went out from the house immediately and told them that they did not belong to me, and that I did not desire their services without making them a compensation."

He gave the crowd a thoughtful, knowing nod, finally acknowledging the effect of his preaching. "Having done this, I felt at liberty to proceed in worship, and returned to my family in the house. After singing, I kneeled to pray. Had I the tongue of an angel, I could not fully describe to you what I felt. All my dejection, and that melancholy gloom which had preyed upon me vanished in a moment, and a divine sweetness ran through my whole frame."

His eyes grew intense now as he met those of the men gathered around him, each in turn. Quietly, he added, "I freed myself from the shackles of Satan when I struck the shackles off of the men and women whom I had oppressed under his evil guidance. It was God, not man, that taught me the impropriety of holding slaves, and I shall never be able to praise Him enough for it. My very heart has bled since that day, both for the slave and the slave-holders, especially those who make a profession of religion, for I believe that it is a crying sin."

Many of the men before him shifted uncomfortably at his words, including Prosper, for they were both slave holders and professed religious feeling, and to hear that this preacher, whose word had appealed so powerfully to them up until this point, felt that they were committing such a grave sin was not what they'd expected to hear that evening.

The preacher could see their unease, and he said, "I do not share my testimony of the Lord's words to me as a means of condemnation, but to impress upon you that there is no shame in ignorance of the enemy's ways of leading us astray in our path to salvation. The Lord perceived that I was ignorant, and so He granted me the guidance I needed. He has further granted me the chance to share this Gospel with you, that you may each escape the Devil's trap of slave-holding."

He smiled, concluding, "I bring you this good news as a gift from our merciful and glorious Lord, that you may join me in the frustration of our enemy's plans."

Several men were making their way to the door to depart, muttering angrily amongst themselves, and Mister Garrettson smiled, calling after them, "The Lord will welcome you back in His boundless mercy, when you repent of your sins, my brothers."

One man shot the preacher a bitter look and called back over his shoulder, "When the Lord is prepared to plow my fields and harvest my crops, I will be happier to hear your Quaker nonsense." Without waiting for Mister Garrettson's reply, he made his way through the door into the inky night beyond.

Mister Garrettson, for his part, turned back to those who remained, and reiterated, "I shall perpetually have an aversion to those who continue the practice of holding our fellow-creatures in abject slavery. It was the blessed God that taught me the rights of man."

He closed his eyes, a somber grimace on his face, before he continued, "I can now tell the present and rising generation that their privileges are very great. In former times in this country, darkness was all around, and now Gospel light breaks forth in every direction. Formerly, the unregenerate were in ignorance, but now they have no cloak for their sins."

He repeated the gesture of seeking out the eyes of each man in his audience, and it seemed to Prosper that when their gazes met, there was a spark that leaped from the preacher into his heart, like a bolt of lightning. The instant passed, though, and Mister Garrettson concluded quietly, "The magnitude of a crime depends greatly upon the light we sin against. I come here not to condemn your former actions, taken in ignorance of that light, but to invite you to follow the Lord's blessed word, and to accept the mercy which He offers us all."

He stepped down from the pulpit, and unlike the last time he'd preached in Mister Stone's barn, he did not remain afterward to pray with the members of the congregation individually, nor to exchange pleasantries as they left.

Like the other men who had not stormed out, Prosper was troubled and thoughtful as he stepped out of the well-lighted space and into the darkness of the night, and did not linger to discuss the sermon with them. He did, however, ponder it as he walked.

If God had spoken to this man and had, in fact, informed him that the holding of slaves was a sin against His light, then the practical questions of how one needed to act were moot. Earthly convenience and pragmatic concerns did not excuse willful acts against God's law.

The angry comment that the one man had made as he departed was, in this view of things, a mere excuse for continued sin. He that had more in common with the man who claimed that he had no choice but to commit theft in order to feed his family, or that the commandment against killing did not apply to a family of

Indians who lived on a parcel of land he coveted. Earthly authority might forgive these sins, but they would still be weighed against a man's soul when he stood before God in the end.

On the other hand, Mister Garrettson's insistence that he had been inspired to this gospel by no other man at all, but by God alone could be just the claims of spiritual authority by someone who had been swayed by the arguments brought forward by the Quakers and other fringe sects, men whose very way of speaking was shaped by their peculiar understanding of God's commandments. Could the preacher have been exposed to those radical ideas in his travels, and have consciously decided that they were of enough import to add them to his own spiritual doctrine?

Or was it possible that God had not so much spoken directly to Mister Garrettson with the unambiguous command the preacher had related to them, as that He had placed into Mister Garrettson's path men who made the arguments against slave-holding so persuasive that it was as if God had given voice to the word?

As his steps retraced the familiar way home, he considered each of these possibilities. The second and third both required that Mister Garrettson should have committed the sin of bearing false witness to one degree or another. While anything was possible, particularly if the Devil had a hand in the preacher's words, it was so much at odds with everything that he'd seen of the man that he was more inclined to seriously consider the first possibility as the most likely.

And if the preacher's sermon had been informed directly by the word of God, revealed to the person of Mister Garrettson, what did that mean for Prosper Creale, and his plantation that already struggled to provide adequately for the needs of his family? If the preacher was to be believed, those concerns arose from the word of Satan, whispered in his ear to draw him away from the light of the Lord's mercy.

Prosper stopped dead in the road, his eyes seeking out the distant pinpricks of the stars in the sky above, but in fact hoping to find the face of God Himself there, as he came to the most consequential realization of his entire life:

God had commanded that his slaves must be set free.

Chapter 9

Arriving home, Prosper said nothing to Kristine, but she took one look at his ashen face and exclaimed, "You look as though you have just seen a ghost abroad in the night!"

He did not want to explain the incredible testimony he had experienced just yet, so he said only, "Something along the road home gave me a fright, but I have made it back to you without suffering any injury." That much was true, at least in the physical sense. Spiritually, and economically, he was uncertain how badly the night's events had harmed him, and he knew it might be some time before that became clear.

She continued to fuss over him, but Prosper dismissed her impatiently. "I have much I need to pray over, and I won't be able to hear even the voice of God over you."

She gave him a wounded look but returned to the hearthside, where she was repairing a shirt that one of the boys had caught on a branch in the woods. Prosper felt a stab of guilt for the harshness of his tone — she was, after all, only concerned for him — but he truly needed some quiet time to contemplate and ask how he was to proceed.

He wondered whether Mister Garrettson had been able to retain the services of his former slaves by offering them wages to continue on at their old jobs. For that matter, how was one to maintain discipline in a workforce that could simply choose to leave, if they did not like their work or its conditions?

His conversation with Cain earlier in the day came back to him, and he wondered how it might have gone, had he not been able to make a credible threat to sell the man, should his behavior not improve. Would the prospect of simply losing his employment, and having to seek some other position, be as effective?

For that matter, the accident that had cost Cato his life had been a simple matter to handle when the man was his property. The biggest concern had been where to bury the unfortunate man's body, instead of any considerations about whether the sheriff might need to take official notice of the death of a man at Prosper's hands.

It would have been easy to demonstrate that Cato's death was an accident, and not even a matter of reckless disregard for the man's safety — but had Cato been a free man, Prosper thought that there would at least have been an inquiry into his death. The disparity between the way a slave's death and that of a free man would be treated only emphasized for Prosper how unjust the practice of slave-holding truly was.

Mister Garrettson had clearly heard the word of God in this matter, and Prosper felt filled with shame that God had not granted him the same boon. Or, was this perhaps what God had meant when He reminded Prosper that to whom much is given, much is required? Had Prosper simply been too focused on his own struggles to understand what the blessed Lord had been trying to tell him?

Then, there were the practical considerations. When he released his hands into freedom, how could he prevail upon them to stay on in their current roles? He must have laborers to tend the fields and get the harvest in — that went without question —

but how would he afford to pay them a wage that would be more appealing to them than striking out on their own?

There was not enough profit in the raising of corn to hire laborers at a rate that might be better than other options available to them, such as joining up in the militia, or going away to sea. As he considered those possibilities, though, he had to acknowledge that the opportunities open to freed slaves were not as wide as those open to a free white man would be. So, perhaps he might not need to offer them as much as he would an ordinary laborer.

Immediately, though, he knew that to leverage this for his own benefit was no less than to engage in a merely attenuated form of slavery, rather than to eliminate it from his plantation entirely as God had commanded. He sighed and stood to fetch a sheet of paper, so that he might put some figures together.

He noticed, as he wrote, that Kristine was paying attention, though she pretended not to be, but he was not yet ready to have the difficult conversation with her that he knew was to come. For the moment, he needed to get the facts clear before his mind, so that he could understand better what God's command to him was going to mean.

He listed the names of each of the slaves in one column, then listed their primary occupation. Beside those, he started writing a neat column of approximate annual wages for a laborer with the skills for that position. He tried to be conservative in his figures, but when he summed up the total, he felt a cold sweat break out over his brow. The number was simply impossibly large. Even with the price increases driven by the disruptions of war, there was hardly anything left.

Still, having figured up the labor expenses he would incur

once he liberated his hands, he wrote down the other expenses on the plantation, and realized that there would be some savings from the change, as well. Once he was paying his hands, he need no longer include a provision for their clothing, or even food, as any other laborer would be expected to pay those costs out of his own wages.

He could even charge the housing that he provided against their wages — again, any other laborer on a plantation would expect the same — so the maintenance of those structures and a reasonable rental charge would be no violation of God's command.

Too, avoiding the large capital expense of buying a new boy to fill the hole in his slaves' ranks left by the loss of Cato, and instead offering the position to all and sundry might cost more over time, but in the short run, it would leave more of his savings intact.

When he got to the income side of his figurings, he again was conservative. Though the disruptions of the conflict with the King had caused prices to increase and had led to the replacement of solid, dependable colonial bills with paper issued by the self-styled Continental Congress, he could not count on that to rescue him from debtor's prison, should he miscalculate.

He narrowed his eyes and put down a figure for each bushel of corn he would harvest that fall, and then multiplied it by the number of bushels he expected his late planting to yield, so long as the weather held. That figure, compared to the costs sum, made his habitual frown deepen into a scowl. The difference between the numbers would leave him with almost nothing in his savings.

He started to look over the list of the hands again, examining each name with closer consideration. Would each of these men earn their keep? Would he make more money by their labors than they would each cost him? And if not, could he even justify keeping them on the plantation?

He started drawing lines through names, hesitating before each one. He would not sell them. No, God's word had been clear, and simply transferring ownership to someone else while pocketing the proceeds would be no less a sin than would be keeping them in bondage, but he could free them and send them off to find their fortunes elsewhere.

He got to Frankie, and his quill hovered over the name, indecision wracking his mind. The old man would not cost very much in wages, and he had served most of his life on the plantation, first under Prosper's father, and then under Prosper. It was also terribly unlikely that anyone else would take him on as a hired hand, at his advanced age.

Prosper re-figured the sum of his costs, in part to procrastinate on making a decision. The other men whose names he'd stricken were young, and had skills that weren't utterly necessary to the success of the plantation, but which should enable them to find employment elsewhere. Frankie, though . . .

He looked at the updated sum and compared it to the number he had projected for the plantation's gross income. They were tantalizingly close together, and if he struck out the per-bushel price and added just a few pence to it, the figures would work out just fine. He made the adjustment and sighed in relief. Prosper could live with this outcome, at least this year.

He looked up from the page to meet Kristine's eyes. He said, without preamble, "God spoke to Mister Garrettson and commanded him to free his slaves. The blessed Lord has also spoken to me directly, and while His commands have not been so clear and direct, I am without doubt that it is God's will that I do likewise."

His wife blanched, and her grip on the shirt fell slack, the garment dropping from her knee to the floor. "Husband, I know that you have been much inspired by the preaching that Mister Garrettson has been doing, and I have said not a single word against him. But your talk of hearing God speak to you is just absurd. And letting that man drive you to ruin our lives is beyond the pale."

Prosper shook his head and held up the page on which he'd been figuring. "It will not ruin our lives to do right by these people, but it will save our souls from eternal domination by the Devil himself."

Kristine scoffed, "So says Mister Garrettson. How do you know that he was not sent by the Devil to tempt good people into throwing away the blessings that God has offered us?"

"When those blessings come on the backs of our fellow creatures, it is not difficult at all to see the hand of Satan in tempting us to seize upon them."

"How can you be certain that these 'fellow creatures,' as you call them, were not placed here by Divine Providence to serve us? Does God not act in many ways that are difficult to comprehend if you do not fully comprehend His plans?"

Prosper stood. "I will not have you accuse me of being a fool, when I tell you that I have heard the voice of God Himself preparing me for this decision. Your duty is to me in helping me to implement the decision that God has thrust upon me."

Kristine's tone grew suspicious. "Why did you not tell me that God had spoken to you, husband?"

He felt somewhat abashed now at not having shared this

momentous event with his wife when it happened. He confessed, "In truth, I had my own doubts as to whether what I had heard was real. However, in hearing the testimony given by Mister Garrettson, I found that the voice I had heard spoke in accord with the word of God as revealed to the preacher's ears."

She made a sour face, and then said, "How convenient that must have seemed."

Prosper's eyes flashed as he shot back at her, "You will not mock me, wife. I am owed your obedience, but more than that, I am owed your respect."

"You shall have my respect so long as your actions in providing for our family deserve it, husband. When you propose to undertake a course of action that can only end in our destitution, even more so in such unsettled days as these, it is my duty to bring your error to your attention, and not to meekly remain silent in some mockery of true respect."

Prosper closed his eyes and took a long, deep breath, trying to calm himself before he answered with more rashness than prudence. With as even a tone as he could muster, he answered her, holding up the paper on which he'd been trying to find answers. "I have been striving to find a course that would let me both answer God's command and ensure the continued well-being of our family, and I believe that I have done so. However, if it meant the loss of our earthly trappings of wealth but would secure our seat beside God on the day of judgment, I would make that bargain without hesitation. I have made the decision to obey the command of God, and I will not argue the question with you further."

Chapter 10

Although he'd decided to follow the command he had received from God, and had told Kristine that he was not willing to argue the point with her, the degree to which his wife doubted his reason still troubled Prosper. It did not help that she refused to speak with him at all when they went to bed.

She turned her back on him after she got into bed and pulled away when he laid his hand on her shoulder. Prosper pursed his mouth and rolled to face away himself, and presently, he could hear her breathing slow and deepen, leaving him alone in wakefulness. He glared into the darkness, doubly irritated at her, both for defying his judgment and for having the audacity to then fall asleep as though she'd done nothing wrong at all.

Prosper fumed silently, rolling back to lie facing the ceiling as she began to snore gently. The running of the household was the extent of her domain; he alone had the responsibility of running the rest of the plantation. She had wanted no house slaves — and he would have been hard-pressed to justify the expense — so the burden of the sin of enslaving creatures little different from himself fell completely upon his shoulders.

She had no legitimate voice in the decision at all. So why was her opposition now keeping him from the peace of sleep?

It was true, certainly, that releasing the hands from bondage would represent the loss of a great deal of capital outlay, and that it might affect the profitability of the operations of the plantation as well. However, if he could rely upon the figures he had arrived at, their annual operations should work out, even with the necessity of paying for the former slaves' labor.

There might not be very much profit, but any number of other disruptions might have also erased their profit overnight. So long as no other financial calamity overcame them, he was confident that they should weather this storm well enough. Of course, he had been worried already about the possibility of disaster, and Kristine had to have been aware of the daily strain it placed him under.

Still, this was his responsibility as the head of the household, and she could only add to his concerns by trying to argue with him about it. Undermining his authority as the decision maker was nearly as bad as simply defying him openly.

He was almost at the point of waking her up to tell her so, when he realized that she was not asleep any longer. His eyes had adapted to the glimmer of light from the moon which shone through the window, so that he could see his wife lying beside him. She still faced away from him, but her shoulders quaked under her shift, and with a shock, he understood that she was sobbing silently. Rolling awkwardly in the bed to face her again, he tried once more to put his hand on her shoulder.

This time, she rolled to face him, her face wet with her tears, and she lay her head on his chest. His arm went automatically around her, offering her comfort, though from what, he wasn't yet certain. She lay like that for a while, her tears soaking through his nightshirt, even as her sobs subsided.

Finally, she said, in a quiet voice interrupted by occasional hiccups, "It may be your privilege to make such momentous decisions for us all, but I should like you to remember, husband, that your decisions will affect us all. If you were to fall into debt and be unable to provide for us at all from a debtor's prison, the children and I would have no place to turn and would have to put ourselves at the mercy of our friends and neighbors."

He started to answer her, but she placed a gentle finger across his lips. "Hush . . . let me finish. If your convictions are strong enough that you feel that you must take that risk, I will allow that it is your place to do so. I will only ask that you consider whether it is just that your children and your wife might bear the cost alongside you, if your figuring is wrong by even a small amount."

Prosper let her words sink in for a long while before he answered. "I would rather risk the possibility of financial reverses, even grievous ones, over the certainty that a failure to act places our souls in peril of punishment in the eternal hereafter. For if the temptations of Satan and his promises of the easy way lead us astray, even our blessed Lord cannot save us from that fate."

He considered for another long moment, and then added, "I know that I did not prepare you for the possibility that I might be driven to make such a choice, when I kept from you the experience of hearing the voice of God with my own senses. It was such a strange and unlikely thing that I still questioned whether I actually experienced it. I did not want to give you cause for concern as to my mind, but I see now that it left you with even more cause to question me."

"It is strange to think that God took the time to trouble Himself with speaking to my own husband," Kristine said, "but if you say that it happened and that you are now satisfied that the experience was genuine, why, then, I believe you. We live in a time when all manner of strange things happen, and given that fact, I can readily enough accept that the Lord has spoken to you and has offered you guidance in this matter."

Prosper gave his wife a squeeze to express his appreciation that she believed him and had not concluded that he had simply taken leave of his senses. She was not finished speaking, however.

"Even so, I must raise the question that presents itself to my mind, husband, and I do so without intending any disrespect. Can you admit the possibility that the voice you heard was instead that of the enemy, trying to direct you toward a path that would result in your being unable to serve God? For if you are imprisoned for debt, and wracked with worry for the fate of your family, does it not follow that your faith might be challenged, and that many men in such circumstances might turn their faces against the blessed Lord entirely, blaming Him for their plight?"

He froze, again frowning into the darkened room as he absorbed her words. A tiny, bright kernel of doubt kindled in his mind as he thought about what she'd said. Could this indeed be one of Satan's subtler tricks? Was the great enemy capable of such a wicked plot in his quest for another soul snatched away from the Lord?

But then he remembered once again the testimony of Mister Garrettson, and his resolve returned to him like the water of a pond seeking its own level after a great rock has splashed it away. There was yet disturbance there, but the firmness of his conviction was restored.

However, he knew he must choose his words carefully, lest he reignite the argument that had spoiled his rest so much already this night. He said, after a long, thoughtful period, "That would be a plot worthy of the evil reputation of the Devil himself, but it would require that the enemy had enlisted the preacher Garrettson in his service, and I find that impossible to believe. Had you met the man, I know you would share my confidence in his testimony, my wife. He is the nearest thing to a true saint that I am likely ever to encounter in this life."

She asked, sharply, "Would you stake your family's security, health, and comfort on your belief in this man's goodness?"

He answered, without hesitation or reservation, "Yes, I would."

He could feel in the tension of her body, rather than see on her face, the frown that marred her face, but she said nothing further, and they fell into an uneasy sleep together at last.

When he awoke with a start to the first light of dawn lighting up the window, he found that she had retreated back to her side of the bed during the night, but there was neither the tense anger, nor the fearful sadness of the prior night in her posture under the blanket. If anything, there was resignation in the slump of her shoulder as she slept, but he admitted to himself that he may have been just interpreting her normal sleeping position in light of the night's disagreements.

Yawning, he swung his legs over the side of the bed and stood. She rolled over, her face puffy and her hair wild despite her cap, and her eyes pinched tightly against the intrusion of the rising sun's light. Scowling, she shook her head, and without opening her eyes, got out of bed on her side.

She said nothing to him as she moved about the room, getting herself prepared for the labors of the day ahead, but this was not unusual. Kristine in the first hour of the morning was not the same person as the Kristine of the latter part of the day, and he had long since learned that it was for the best if he just left her to her own devices when they rose.

He quietly drew on his trousers and put his hair into a tidy club. With a thrill of excitement, he remembered he had an important conversation ahead of him this day, and the prospect of informing the hands that he was granting them their freedom gave his every step a new urgency.

Coming down the stairs, he found Tace sitting beside the cats' bed, chuckling to herself with delight at their antics. Prosper remembered his wife's question from the night before and, as he looked at his daughter's face beaming with joy, he wished he could completely extinguish the doubt Kristine had planted. Were there not mortal sins that he would commit to ensure the safety of his family, to preserve the cheerful giggle that followed him into the front hall?

He was no Abraham, being called upon to sacrifice his own child on the altar of God, and yet, was he not being called upon in like manner to risk sacrificing some part of her in the service of the Lord? Yet, if no angel appeared to offer a lamb in substitute, was that proof that the risk he feared would not materialize?

He shook his head to himself, grimacing. There was no need to make the matter any more complex than it already was. The simple fact was that the Lord had commanded that he must set his slaves free, and so he must follow that command. He could drape it in as much confusion as he liked, but in the end, he had to recognize that the additional layers were offered to his mind not by God, but by the Devil. He could safely ignore them — indeed, he had to cast them aside, leaving only the clear word of God.

He drew on his boots and buckled them, rehearsing in his mind what he must say to the hands, in order to introduce the concept of their freedom to them, without causing them undue worry for the security and stability of their lives. Hesitating for a moment, he left the serviceable but stained old coat on its peg, and took instead his Sunday coat. This was, after all, going to be the most important day in his slaves' lives, and he ought to honor them with the best appearance he could manage.

Finally, Prosper Creale donned his hat, squared his shoulders, and opened the door to step out into the light of the new day dawning on his plantation.

Chapter II

The hands stood gathered before him, summoned into the barn by Primus, with help from the younger boys among them. He surveyed the group, took a deep breath, and began.

"You men have served me to the best of your abilities, some of you for many years, and it is only fitting that I should express to you how much I appreciate your labors over that time. I know all too well that it is not by your own will that you have done your work, and that I have taken my full part in the custom of our society and laws to bind you to the labor that I required."

He could see several of the men shifting uneasily, fear visible on their faces, and he wondered for an instant what could have frightened them. Then he realized that they must be thinking that he meant to sell them, and he hurried to continue.

"Our blessed Lord spoke to me through a preacher I went and listened to last night, and that man testified that He had said that the practice of keeping our fellow-creatures in bondage was a sin and must be ended at once."

Prosper saw a couple of the brighter men start to comprehend what he was saying, their eyes lighting up in anticipation. "Therefore, I am freeing all of you at once, and will offer those of you such as choose to continue in your current employment the fairest wages I can for your labors."

He motioned at the fields visible behind him through the barn door. "I cannot raise this crop without most all of you helping me, nor would it be an easy thing to find new hands to hire, should you choose to leave. However, as of this moment, if you do not wish to continue to serve me on this plantation, you are free to go."

Cain grinned and stepped out from behind the men who had partially concealed him in the group. "I'll be glad for my walking papers, Mister Creale."

Prosper nodded gravely. "And you shall have them, just as soon as I can draw them up." Inwardly, he felt a return of the clutch of fear that had come upon him when he'd first considered the practical aspects of this action. He had been counting on Cain staying, and filling that capable man's shoes would be an immediate challenge.

Another man stepped forward, and a third. Both had been men whose names he'd stricken from his list already, so he was well enough satisfied that they were willing to leave of their own accord.

To his surprise, Frankie glanced around, and then stepped tentatively over to the smaller group. Prosper's face must have betrayed his feelings, for the old man smiled and offered him an explanation.

"My brother lives not twenty miles from here, but I have not seen him since we were younger than Mister Cain, there. I have had word of him over the years, and I do believe that he would be glad enough to take me in. In any event, I should like to see him again before I start my new life as a free man."

Prosper nodded in acknowledgment. "If your brother cannot provide for you, or you do not find employment at a wage that will permit you to provide for yourself, I would be happy to welcome you back here."

Looking over the remaining men, he called out three of their names. "With needing to pay fair wages to those I must have in order to continue to work this plantation, I must reduce your numbers to the absolute minimum. I will vouch for your work as you seek employment elsewhere, but I cannot justify keeping you on."

One man, Phineas, cried out, "But Mister Creale, who will hire a negro, whether or not he is a free man?"

Prosper said solemnly, "You may have heard that there is a war underway between these colonies and the mother country. Many men from this region have joined the militia to take up arms in defense of what they imagine to be our freedoms and have left much work undone in their absence."

He tried to make his smile as reassuring as possible. "I have every confidence that you will all find employment before the fortnight is over. I will not turn you out of your lodgings with no time to prepare, but neither can I afford to feed and clothe you indefinitely. If you will continue at your labors, I will permit you to stay for one month, but after that time, you will need to have found another arrangement."

Cain spoke up now, saying, "Don't you worry none, Mister Phineas. You come on with me, and the lot of us will offer ourselves up as an experienced team, accustomed to working together."

Prosper gave his former slave a grateful smile, and said, "Mister Cain, I wish you the very best that our merciful God can bestow upon you and your companions. If you will wait by the house, I will go and draw up your manumissions now, so that you can all be on your way."

Turning back to the group who were, — for the moment at least — staying, he said, "You may return to your accustomed tasks now, but know that I will pay you for your labors. I will speak to each of you individually today to discuss the terms of your continued employment here, and to answer your questions."

He spread his hands out in benediction. "I give you all the joy of your freedom."

Gathering up the group who were leaving with a motion of his chin, he returned to the house. On the broad porch, he said, "You may take your ease here, while I draw up your papers. Missus Creale does not necessarily agree with my doing this, and so I would not like to provoke her by inviting you into the house."

Cain sauntered over to a bench beside the door and settled down at once. The other men found seats, as well, though most of them looked more ill at ease than did Cain.

Prosper entered the house, shaking his head at having lost Cain's leadership on the plantation, but determined to follow through on his word. He went to the study and drew out several clean pages. He hesitated for a long moment, and then began to write.

"Know all men by these presents that I, Prosper Creale, of Charles County, Maryland Colony, do hereby manumit, emancipate, and set free the Negro man known as Cain and release to him all my right and claim to his labor and future earnings. Witness my hand and seal on this date."

He signed and dated the page with a flourish, and then set the document aside to work through the rest, referring to the wording of the first as he went, so that they would all be consistent. Arranging the stack so that he could work with each page in turn, he lit a taper and heated the sealing-wax over its flame.

Affixing his seal to each page, he set them aside to finish cooling, and extinguished the flame. He gazed at the stack of papers, trying to put the thought of the total value they represented out of his mind. He had this morning reduced his estate by over half, and these pages were but the formal acknowledgment of the beginning of that process.

He wondered briefly whether this was enough to satisfy God's reminder to him that much was expected from a man to whom much had been given. He sat back in his seat, realizing that the labor that he had been by force from these men certainly qualified as being much given.

Any lingering doubts he had in his mind about whether he was taking the course that God had intended for him vanished in that moment, and he stood, his resolution strengthened by the thought.

Prosper folded each of the pages and wrote the corresponding man's name on the outside and then emerged from his study with the manumissions in his hand. He found Kristine standing at the doorway to the kitchen, her arms crossed. He stopped and waited to hear what she had to say.

She regarded him with a frown, but said nothing, turning back to enter the kitchen and continue her work there. Though the argument was settled now that he had spoken to the hands and had started writing out their manumissions, he knew that it was far from over.

Outside, he handed each man his paper, and took a moment to speak with Cain. "I know that you and I came to be at odds of late, and I do not hold against you your decision to quit this place and seek your fortune elsewhere. I ask that you not lead these men into any sort of trouble, both for your own sakes, as well as for mine."

He nodded toward the village. "There will be plenty of men who do not understand why I felt compelled to give you all your freedom, and if you make poor use of it, they may come to hold me to account for your actions. Many of them will not share my feeling that we are fellow men under God, but instead will see you as my wayward property. Do you understand?"

Cain nodded, although he was frowning. "I will speak my mind, Mister Creale, since you say that you now believe us to be fellow men. I do not care what any man says, if he thinks that I am just an animal to be bought and sold."

He tapped his manumission on his chest for emphasis. "This here paper says otherwise, and any man who does not believe it can answer to your God, as far as I am concerned."

Prosper nodded in agreement. "Yet you ought to bear in mind that most of the people of this community will find the idea of a free Negro man to be both foreign and fearful. It is not just, but it is a fact."

Cain nodded toward the other men. "I will keep us all out of trouble. Mister Frankie is a good influence, and the rest of them are good boys. You need not worry on our account."

The habits of a lifetime kept Prosper from offering the other hand his hand as they parted, but he did wave to them after they'd stepped down off the porch. Their bearing reflected a range of emotions — from Cain, who stood tall and proud, to Phineas, who still looked fearful and anxious — but they lined up as though in a work crew on their way to a task, and set out onto the road, each clutching the paper that had put them on their own path. None of them had any belongings more precious than that, and the habits of slavery precluded extended farewells.

Prosper watched them as they went around the bend in the road, and then took a deep breath and went out to seek out Primus and acquaint him with the new terms of his employment.

By the time he walked into the kitchen for dinner, he had spoken with each of the men remaining on the plantation, and had handed each of them their manumissions, telling them the wage he intended to offer them and answering their questions.

Jack had wanted to know whether he would be able to visit his friends at Mister Wrangell's place. "You ought to get Mister Wrangell's permission to set foot on his property, but your movements are your own business, as far as I am concerned. I will expect you to be at your duties for which I am paying you, but outside of those hours, your time is your own." Jack nodded and seemed satisfied, and slipped his manumission into his shirt before returning to his work.

When Prosper handed the last man his walking papers, he waited for a moment to see whether he felt the same lifting of his spirit that Mister Garrettson had described. All he felt was weariness, and the satisfaction of a hard job well done. God's voice remained silent in his ears, but he felt increasingly certain that this had been the Lord's will from the first moment He had spoken to him.

Prosper was pleased to see that they had, to a man, been more dedicated than ever to the tasks he had assigned. The prospect of being paid for their labor seemed to motivate them far more than the fear of being disciplined for their failure. That factor had not been a part of his figurings the prior night, and it gave him hope things might work out, after all.

He needed that hope in the face of Kristine's terse silence. Although she'd said that she would acquiesce to his decision, now that he had executed it beyond the power to revoke, he could tell that she was resentful of the relinquishment of so much property at one fell swoop.

He sat and looked around the table at his family. Tace and Phillip gazed back, their solemn expressions echoing the mood that they sensed from their parents. The older boys, Humility and Clement, sat side-by-side, oblivious to the upsets of their parents, eager to return to the woods and whatever project they were working on there together.

Faith and Hope, both nearly husband-high, and blooming with the advancing springtime, were exchanging whispers that fell silent at a glare from their mother.

"Unto whomsoever much is given, of him shall be much required." The voice sounded in his ear again, but this time, it seemed to Prosper that it had a tone of approval, instead of command.

And this time, he did not react outwardly, other than to lowered his head and give the blessing for dinner. He murmured, "Let us thank our blessed Lord for this day and for this meal, and for the gifts we each have been given. But most of all, let us thank our Redeemer for the duties He lays upon us, that we may joyfully demonstrate our gratitude by our acts. Please, oh Lord, continue to guide our family to more closely follow in Your path. In the holy name of Your son Jesus, Amen."

An urgent rap at the door interrupted the moment of silence. Prosper and Kristine glanced at each other, and he rose to answer.

Chapter 12

Rising from the table, Prosper found Mister Wrangell at the door, an expression of mixed disbelief and anger on his face. Mastering his irritation at being interrupted at the dinner table, Prosper asked, "What may I do for you, neighbor?"

"I encountered a gaggle of your negroes out abroad on the road, and they told me the most curious tale. I was so perplexed at it that I was moved to come and speak to you without delay."

Prosper nodded. "Go on."

"They claimed that God told you that you must release all of your slaves from bondage, and they even had certificates of manumission that they claimed you had prepared for them. They are not witnessed or recorded, but they gave every appearance of being in your hand, friend, and the matter troubled me deeply."

"Those men told you nothing but the truth, Mister Wrangell. I was moved by the testimony the Mister Garrettson gave last night, and by my own encounters with the voice of our blessed Lord. I determined that the only means by which I could escape from the grave sin of which I had become sensible that I was committing was to follow Mister Garrettson's example and immediately set free my fellow-creatures whom I had previously held in bondage."

Wrangell's face underwent a remarkable series of contortions, starting with an expression of open disbelief, and proceeding to a tight grimace of apparent anger, before he shook his head and demanded, "And how do you suppose my negroes will receive this news, Mister Creale? Did you stop to ponder the impact that your actions will have upon your neighbors and the rest of your community?"

Prosper started to answer, but Wrangell spoke right over him, continuing, "How are these freed slaves supposed to provide for themselves, or are you satisfied that they should maraud over the countryside, taking what they need from all and sundry, like an invading army?"

Prosper did not give the other man a chance to continue, firing back, "Did you bother to ask those men about their intentions? They are good, capable hands, all of them, and they represented to me that they planned to offer their labor to any who might need it. I have enough here without them, and so I gave them leave to pursue that plan without my interference."

He raised a finger to emphasize his point. "You, sir, have tried and convicted them within the dark precincts of your own mind, without giving these men the chance to demonstrate any hint of ill intent. Your suspicions of them are without cause." He dropped his hand and made an effort to calm himself before he was moved to say more.

His neighbor's scowl deepened. "Even if they behave as perfect lambs, do you suppose for a moment that my hands will not demand to know why these men are set free, while they yet serve at my command?"

Prosper raised his palms and shrugged slightly. "That must be a matter between you and God, my friend. I am following what I understand to be His commands, and I can only urge you to escape, likewise, from the sin of holding your fellow creations of God in bondage against His will."

Wrangell's scowl turned even stormier, and he retorted, "I should think that one plantation owner winding up in prison for debt should be quite enough for this area. I will not follow you into madness and ruin, sir, no matter how much you dress it up in holier-than-thou language."

Prosper nodded placidly. "I do not expect you to take my word that this is God's will, but I would encourage you to keep your mind and ears open for the evidence that He may offer you of that will."

"God does not present Himself to the likes of you or me," Wrangell scoffed. "Whatever the true source of your madness, I only hope that it does not bring disaster to those of us who must witness it. In the meantime, I would take it as a kindness if you would ask your hands to keep their distance from my slaves. I don't need this mental infirmity of yours spreading to give them cause for dissatisfaction and unrest."

Prosper nodded, signaling his acquiescence. "This will come as hard news to my man Jack, who has friends among your hands, but I will pass it along to him."

Wrangell looked startled for a moment, and then said, "Oh, Jack is all right, I suppose, so long as you can prevail upon him to not cause any trouble with my hands. He's come around plenty of times before, and no harm has come of it. For that matter, my house servant Sally was asking after your Cato, to whom she is apparently quite attached. That was some weeks back, though, so I don't know whether their connection is still a continuing matter."

Prosper sighed deeply. "Cato lost his life in an accident

nearly a month ago. I was told that he had a woman among your hands, but I presumed that one of my men would have passed the word of Cato's loss on to her."

Wrangell looked surprised at the news, and then shrugged. "Perhaps someone did. Cato always struck me as a good negro. I am sorry for your loss. Did that have something to do with your decision to free the rest of them?"

Prosper shook his head. "No, I was driven to that purely by the word of God, as I said. The circumstances of Cato's death brought me great sadness, but it was solely the word of God that persuaded me."

"As you say," Wrangell replied, his tone still skeptical. "I apologize for my sharp words earlier. I am truly concerned about the outcome of this experiment of yours, and worried about the effect it may have on the rest of us in the area."

"No apology is needed, my friend. I know you spoke from genuine feeling, and not mere resistance to change. As for the effects upon those in the area, why, you may find that Cain and his fellows are of some use around your plantation, should your labor be short of what you need. They are all well-skilled and hardworking, and I will likely offer them work in the busiest part of the season myself."

Wrangell frowned. "I still don't think that it's a good idea to bring free negroes into proximity to my hands, lest they become jealous and desire me to offer them the same station. I have not the resources to dispose of half my wealth so casually as you have done."

He narrowed his eyes and frowned again. "This is still going to make matters more difficult for all the rest of us. I hope you know what you're doing, and that you do not wind up costing us all dear."

With that, he turned, waving a somewhat civil farewell over his shoulder. Prosper returned the gesture and closed the door, returning to his dinner table, where Kristine gave him a curious look.

"It was just Mister Wrangell, sharing his thoughts about the changes I have made here."

Clement looked up from his plate, which was already more than halfway to being empty. "What changes, Pa?"

Prosper explained to his eldest son, "The hands are now free men, and are employed in their former jobs for wages at their own sufferance, rather than under the lash."

Humility gaped openly over his brother's shoulder at Prosper, and Clement swallowed hard before asking, slowly, "Is this because of Governor Dunmore's proclamation? Are you trying to forestall our slaves from running off to fight for the Virginia loyalists?"

"Nay," said Prosper, startled. "The thought had not so much as entered my mind, to be honest. After all, that is over in Virginia, and none of our men has ever showed any interest in taking up arms for the King, anyway."

Humility spoke up now. "Mister Armstrong had two slaves run off last month, and it was said that they were bound for Lord Dunmore's army."

Prosper pursed his mouth in disapproval. It was not unusual for the boys to be better-informed as to the gossip around town, but it disturbed him that they thought that he had undertaken this course of action as a cynical means of forestalling any runaways from the plantation's hands.

Kristine broke in, her tone outwardly neutral, but Prosper thought he detected a hint of archness in it. "God Himself directed your father to set our slaves free, in order to preserve his soul from an awful sin."

The boys turned back to Prosper, their heads swiveling in unison, in a manner that might have made him laugh aloud at another time.

He nodded gravely, though, keeping his features composed. "The blessed Lord was merciful enough to provide me with instruction when He discerned that I had strayed into error and sin, and I had little choice but to follow the guidance that He offered."

"But . . . will we have enough hands to do all the work around here?" Clement's face bore an expression of concern.

"Oh, aye, and indeed, I dismissed a few, beyond those who opted to seek their fortunes elsewhere."

It was Faith's turn to look worried. "What will they do with themselves?"

"I very much doubt that they will have any trouble finding work, with so many men called to duty in the militia. They are all strong, capable men, and they have skills that will apply to nearly any plantation in the colony."

Humility asked, "Who all left us?"

Prosper named the men who had departed, and Humility gasped aloud when he got to Cain. "Why, Cain was supposed to help us build a cabin in the woods next week, and now you tell us he is gone, just like that?"

"Aye, he was one of those who chose to go his own way, and the word of God commanded me to permit him to follow his own wishes with no restriction, and to give him leave to pursue any lawful business that he might see fit." Prosper hesitated, and then added, "Cain is one of many whom I wish had stayed, but it was not my place to force him into labor that is not of his own will."

He opted not to mention the conflict between Cain and Primus, though he felt sure that it had been a part of Cain's decision to strike out on his own.

Humility's shoulders drooped, and he said to Clement, "I suppose we shall just have to build the cabin by ourselves, though it will not be as good as what Cain would have been able to do with us."

Prosper said, "You might also be able to persuade one of the other men to help you, after their work for the day is completed."

"Or on Sunday," Clement said, too quickly to be interrupted by his brother's elbow in his ribs.

Prosper frowned. "You ought keep the Sabbath for prayer and reflection, boys, and leave the hands to do likewise."

"Yes, sir," they said in unison, but Prosper recalled all too clearly how tempting Sunday afternoons could be for adventures and projects. He did not actually expect that they would follow his lead in reserving Sunday for conversations with God.

With no further questions arising for a moment, he took the opportunity to dig into the dinner that Kristine had prepared. It was some sort of stew with a few stringy bits of chicken in it — doubtless some hen that had outlived her egg-laying days — but hardly any seasoning outside of salt. As he chewed and swallowed, more out of habit than any actual hunger, he wondered idly whether she was trying to register a continued protest against his decision, through the very food on his plate. If so, it was no more than a tepid protest.

He finished the meal with only a couple more interruptions. The boys wanted to know if he thought that they could pay Cain to help them with their cabin — Prosper said that he did not have the money to spare on such a project — and Hope asked what arrangements the departed men might have made for lodging. Prosper shrugged and said that it was their responsibility as free men to find suitable solutions to all the problems of providing for themselves.

Explaining to Tace the difference between Cato going away permanently and Cain going away, but still being around the community was the most challenging of these. He thought that he might have finally made it clear to her when he compared Cato's departure to that of one of the kittens — the runt — which had died a few days after they were born, and the tomcat which had gone out to visit some other farm, but which would undoubtedly return as usual after a few days.

The concept of death was obviously still one that she didn't quite believe in, and Prosper let it go at the explanation that she might see both Cato and the lost kitten after the end of her own life, but that she could expect to see both Cain and the tomcat well before then.

Chapter 13

After dinner, Prosper went back out to check on the hands' progress at picking weeds out of the big field. He found Jack bent at his job, methodically pulling anything that was not a corn stalk out from between the rows.

"I am glad to see you, Mister Creale," he called out, barely looking up from his task. "You said that you would continue to let us live in the quarters here, and you would pay for our food out of our wages, but what of the food that we raise for our own selves?"

"That's a fair question, Jack. If you can raise enough food by your own efforts that I don't have to buy anything for you, why then, you can keep that portion of your wages. However, because you all live and eat together, it would have to be for the lot of you, rather than just one or two."

Jack nodded. "That seems fair. What about our quarters? If we maintain those ourselves, with no costs to you, would you be able to pay us that part of our wages in money, as well?"

Prosper paused to think for a moment before answering. "I think I should still have to charge you something for the ground rent, at least, as well as something fair for the use of the structure."

"But we built the quarters ourselves, mostly out of logs that we hauled ourselves from the woods. The only thing you had to pay for was a couple of hinges from the blacksmith." He added, thoughtfully, "We could even argue that we paid for those already with our labor."

Prosper thought of his figures and their tight tolerances, with no real room for error. Then he conceded the point with a grin. "You have me there, Jack. I'll tell you what. I'll have Primus talk it over with you all, to make sure that everyone is satisfied with an arrangement that has me paying you all your full wages — but I will warn you that in order to make this work, I will need to be certain that I can bring a superior crop to market this autumn. If we fall short there, I will be ruined, and a ruined man cannot pay any wage at all."

Jack said, without hesitation, "I will do my best to deliver on that deal, sir, and I feel certain that the other men will do the same."

A smile quirked on Prosper's lips. "I will pray to God that your best is enough to overcome the chances of weather and fate."

Walking away from the man, he couldn't help but wonder whether he had made a mistake in conceding so quickly on the question of their quarters. It was true that the hands had constructed their own quarters, and the only meaningful way in which it had been at his expense was if he considered their labor as his right of ownership . . . and that was the whole crux of the problem to begin with.

They had been his property at the time, even if that state of bondage was counted as a sin against his soul. Was he obliged to pay them fair wages for all of the time that they had worked for him, and not just from the moment that he had freed them? This was not a question of the law — that was squarely on his side, should he simply say that he had owned their labor prior to today — but rather of interpreting God's word to him.

He sighed. He suspected that if God were to speak to him again, He would say that these men were owed compensation for their time in bondage and more, but there seemed no way to satisfy that requirement that did not lead directly to the debtor's prison, and a pauper's grave. Would God demand such an outcome as an earthly punishment for the sin he had unknowingly committed by keeping these men in bondage?

That did not comport with the fact that he was the servant of a merciful and gracious God, nor was it expected that sin should be punished in this life, without the possibility of earning redemption through the blood of Jesus.

He remembered the vivid picture that Mister Garrettson had given of being sensible of two spirits vying for his soul as they each argued their case to him, and he wondered if it had felt to the preacher the way that this argument felt to him.

Absent any further direct guidance from God, he decided that he should lay the question before his fellow man, and seek the advice of his friend Mister Stone, who had played host to Mister Garrettson's last two meetings. Perhaps he would have some insight that had eluded Prosper.

He stopped in at the house to inform Kristine that he was going to seek advice on a business matter before he started out to the woodworker's shop. She said nothing, only nodding, but he could practically hear her arch reply just from the expression on her face. She obviously thought that he should have sought advice the day before.

Nearly halfway to Mister Stone's shop, he found Cain and the others on the road, looking dejected and confused. Prosper called out as he approached, "Good afternoon to you, Mister Cain.

I had thought that you would all have been halfway to Mister Frankie's brother's plantation by now."

Cain replied, the morning's optimism and excitement completely absent in his tone. "We would have been, Mister Creale, except that we could find no place to work the day in exchange for lodgings for the night, nor any employment that would let us simply pay for a place to sleep. We were coming back to your plantation to ask you what we ought to do."

"Did you find nobody who was willing to even offer you so much as guidance?" As soon as he asked the question, Prosper knew it was a foolish one. An unannounced group of negroes, with nothing more to their name than their manumissions, would not have been a welcome sight anyplace that he could think of.

Cain looked miserable as he answered solemnly, "No, sir. Everyone we spoke to assumed that we had run off, and even when we showed them the proof of our freedom, they told us to just be on our way, though the exact words they used were often more wicked than that."

Prosper frowned, imagining just how wicked the comments these men had endured must have been. Turning his eyes heavenward, he asked God to give him some answer to the quandary posed by the plight of his former slaves, but the Lord did not see fit to speak at that moment, and Prosper was left to his own devices.

Sighing, he said, "I was just going to Mister Stone's shop to discuss a related matter, and you may accompany me, if you like. Perhaps he will have some useful insights for us all."

"Yes sir, thank you." Cain gathered up the other former slaves with a quick gesture, and they fell into step behind Prosper as he started off for Mister Stone's shop again.

The odd procession drew attention as they neared the village, and Prosper could see men making whispered comments to one another as they passed. The only one he could hear was one man remarking to another, "I heard that he's completely taken leave of his senses, what with one thing and another." His companion shushed him noisily, and Prosper could not even tell which of them had spoken as he turned to glare at them. Neither of them offered him even an acknowledgment, and he turned back to the road ahead, his customary frown deeper than usual.

Turning down the lane on which Mister Stone's shop lay, the absurd appearance of their group reflected in the window of a house they were passing finally made Prosper's scowl fade. The lengthening shadows that preceded them along the road erased the difference between former master and former slave, leaving them all alike in their shambling humanity. When his own stumble on a branch was echoed by the shadow of one of the men behind him, Prosper couldn't help but chuckle aloud.

He turned to apologize to the man who'd stumbled, not wanting to look as though he were laughing at the misfortune of another. Phineas smiled ruefully, saying only, "I saw you trip in the same place, and should have been looking better to see what you tripped on."

Cain observed dryly, "We are all victims of the same hazards in the end, ain't we?"

"Indeed," Prosper agreed, turning back to lead the way and look out for any further obstacles on their path. Rapping on Mister Stone's shop door when they arrived, he wondered for a moment what that man would make of his sudden appearance with so many others, unannounced at his doorstep.

Once again, Stone was at the door almost immediately, and invited them all inside without asking any questions beforehand, holding the door open wide in welcome.

"What brings you here with such a large team, Mister Creale? Do you mean to purchase an entire plow's worth of lumber from me?"

"Nay," Prosper said, "I intend to ask for something far more dear: your advice as a fellow man of religious conviction."

Stone's eyebrows rose, but he said nothing, motioning the men to a pair of long benches and a set of chairs. Prosper sat in one of the chairs, and Mister Stone took a seat facing him.

Without further preamble, Prosper explained, "In the wake of Mister Garrettson's testimony of the other night, I was deeply troubled at the fact that God had told him to free his slaves, and yet I still held mine in bondage. I asked the dear Lord for some sign of how I was to proceed, and He gave me the clearest impression that I ought to follow Mister Garrettson's example."

Mister Stone shot him a surprised look, seeming to anticipate Prosper's next statement.

"In consequence, I have manumitted every one of the men who I had held as a slave and have offered most of them employment for wages. These men with me either declined my offer or were among those whose services I determined I could not afford."

"This is a most Godly act, my friend, and I must admit that I am quite surprised that Mister Garrettson's sermon had so immediate and marked effect upon your soul." He smiled gently, shaking his head. "There are many among our erstwhile congregation who have told me in no uncertain terms that they do not wish to hear such testimony from Mister Garrettson nor any other man ever again."

Prosper nodded. "Though the wages of sin are death, there are many who cannot see that they are imperiling their souls in the hereafter for the prospect of a few extra shillings to ease their earthly concerns."

"Mister Garrettson himself could hardly have put it better, my friend. But surely you did not come here with these men merely to tell me of your deeds?"

"Nay, I did not. I came to seek your counsel on a matter that has proceeded from the original act of manumission, and these men have come with me for a similar purpose. Having heard Mister Garrettson's testimony, I had hoped that you might be able to help me see some way forward in both matters."

Mister Stone spread his broad, scarred hands. "I will do my best, my friends, though I am but a woodworker, and no carpenter such as our blessed Savior was."

Prosper smiled at the man's witticism, and then first explained the difficulty he faced in accounting for the past sins of claiming ownership of other men and their labor. He concluded with the question, "Do you suppose that the Lord demands that I ought to compensate the victims of my past misdeeds for the time before I was awakened to their sinful nature?"

Mister Stone looked thoughtfully at the group, pulling at his lip as he considered. Finally, he said, "Imagine, Mister Creale, that you were in a state of innocence as to the nature of all sin, and were conducting yourself according to your own lights, with no understanding of God's will."

Prosper frowned slightly, but nodded. "Men who have

not been granted the boon of hearing the Gospel commonly find themselves in such a state."

"Exactly, and God does not specifically condemn them for it, but only seeks to bring the good news of Jesus' sacrifice to such unfortunate souls before the opportunity of salvation has eluded them entirely."

Prosper spread his hands before himself to indicate that he followed Stone's line of thought. "And having done so, if they choose to hear the word of God, the Lord forgives all."

Mister Stone's expression bore approval, and he answered, "Just so. Now, having imagined a person in such a state of innocence, but who has sinned unknowingly against the word of God, bringing harm to another in the process. Earthly authority may be blind to that harm, but the eyes of God see all. Once our imagined person confessed his sins, what is the commandment that is offered to him?"

"Go forth and sin no more."

"Yes, exactly, and his past sins are washed away in that moment in the eyes of God. What our imagined sinner does about the harm he might have once caused is a matter for his own conscience, and for the temporal authority, should it take notice."

Prosper thought for a long time about what Mister Stone has said. Finally, he said, slowly, "Our temporal authority will take no notice of the harm I have caused to these men and their fellows on my plantation, but that offers no balm to my conscience, else I would not have sought your advice. Thank you for helping me to see that."

He turned to his former slaves, looking over their range of dull, dejected expressions. He thought about the saved money in his purse at home, and about the life he was trying to provide for his children. There seemed no possible path he could take that would permit him to satisfy all of the competing priorities he needed to balance.

"Of him, much will be required." Prosper couldn't be sure whether he was just recalling the last time he had heard the words in his mind, or whether God had spoken again to remind him, but in either case, the message was clear enough.

He stood, and said to his former slaves, "Come on back with me, and I will make this right for you, whatever I need to do. There is more that I owe you than merely your walking papers, and I mean to give it to you."

Chapter 14

With Kristine sound asleep beside him, Prosper lay awake, staring at the ceiling, only dimly visible in the moonlight reflecting from outside the window. Doing only what God commanded, and no more, was no way into the blessed hereafter, and he supposed he had always known that.

The practical problems of how to deliver upon his promise to make up to the men he had enslaved for his past misdeeds seemed intractable. If he tried to figure up how much a fair wage would be for each of the men he had held in bondage, his head soon spun with the dizzying totals he arrived at.

There didn't seem to be enough money in his world to satisfy that sort of debt to them, and any attempt to do so out of his farm's earnings could lead only to him being taken up for debts to other men.

His holdings were considerable, even with their reduction with the manumission of the slaves he'd owned, but converting the value of the land into sufficient money was the work of many patient years, if not decades, and had in the past relied on paying only for the acquisition of laborers, not the ongoing value of their labor.

The tools and work animals he owned did not amount to much in the face of such an enormous debt, and the few fine things around the house were so precious to Kristine that the idea of causing her to part with them — even if they had held enough value to be significant — only crossed his mind for an instant before he rejected it out of hand. She was already unhappy enough with him, without embittering her by taking away what little had brought her joy.

Providing settlements for Faith, Hope, and Tace, as well as legacies for the boys, required that he bend all his efforts toward increasing the value of his estate, but if he fell short in that regard, it would but make their lives a bit more difficult than they might otherwise have been. His own father had not left him a substantial legacy, but he had done well enough to this point.

On the other hand, the living means of his success, the men who slept now in their quarters, would not merely struggle, but would likely literally starve to death, if he did not do for them what his conscience cried out for him to do. His realization in Mister Stone's shop that he owed them some sort of compensation for their service prior to being freed had been perfectly clear, even if the way to accomplish it had not been.

In a flash of inspiration, Prosper realized what he had been overlooking, and he gave thanks instantly to the Lord for letting him see the solution that had been literally sitting before his face. The answer lay in the woods.

The same woods where his boys loved to play, and where they wanted to construct a cabin for themselves, formed a substantial part of the overall land holdings that Prosper had inherited, several hundred acres at the least. Much of the land which he had converted already to agriculture had been his own additions to the family estate, while the challenge of clearing the woods for other purposes had always seemed like a distant priority.

However, the land was not without value, even if it was not ready for immediate use, and there was a lot for him to work with. If he offered each of his former slaves an acre for each year of their service to him, it should enable each to have enough land to make a decent living. He would need to do the figures to be sure that he actually had enough land to make such a settlement with them, but that could be a problem for the morning.

At the very least, he could make that offer to the men who had left his service. What they did with the land was up to them, of course. If they wanted to try their luck elsewhere, they could sell the land, but if they preferred to stay put, they could develop their own smallholdings and even establish families.

As he was relaxing into sleep, a fresh worry occurred to him, though. Would the laws even permit negroes to own property? He felt quite certain that they would not be granted the privileges of voting that white men who owned sufficient property gained, but could he even record a transfer of real estate to former slaves?

He knew he was already going to be considered eccentric for having released his hands from bondage, but if he was to find a way to compensate them properly for their service to him over the years, he might have to become downright radical.

His dreams were troubled, and unlike most mornings, he recalled them with the vivid intensity of his waking hours, so much so that it took him several minutes after he woke to convince himself that they had not been real. Like most dreams, though, there were some elements of them that did not make sense in the real world.

The whimsy of the first remembered dream brought a gentle smile to his face, but the next one erased it entirely. Even energetic young cats such as the litter that now bounced around the house to Tace's delight, did not join forces to fetch a full-sized hat from the peg on the wall and then wear it, having somehow altered it in the process so that it would fit them.

Nor did a slave — even a former slave — take to the pulpit to preach a sermon on the advantages of slavery, and to suggest that God would not have permitted slavery to come about if it had not been His will that some should serve and others should command. Prosper had no trouble at all in detecting the hand of the devil in suggesting this pernicious idea to his sleeping mind, and he shook his head to dispel the violent rebellion he had experienced in his mind in response to the illusory sermon.

The final dream that he could recall — the one from which he awoke — was the most surreal of the lot, and he pondered on it as he went through the motions of his morning ablutions. It had taken place in the course of the discussion that followed most sermons he had attended, but it was thankfully not the sermon that had caused him such upset.

The details of the sermon itself eluded him, as was so often the case with dreams that left traces of memory in his mind, but the conversation had centered on the question of whether a correct path followed by good men for bad reasons was as worthy as an equally correct path followed by bad men for good reasons. He and the preacher were dissecting the theological underpinnings of the question.

The preacher had been in the process of reminding him that Satan had once been an angel, and that men could be inspired by the devil to do things that seemed to arise from an angelic source, and that those actions might even seem at first examination to be correct.

Prosper could tell that he was on the verge of citing the infamous question of how many angels could dance on the head of a pin, but that the other man was stuck in trying to find a way to make that question relevant when Cato had joined in the discussion, startling Prosper into losing the thread of his argument entirely.

He interrupted the preacher in the middle of what he was saying and turned to Cato. "Have you some report from the hereafter?"

"Oh, it's a fine place, Mister Creale, and they are full of joy to see what you have done since I left here."

"They have time to take note of my affairs?"

"There's no hurry for anything, no, sir, so there's always a moment to look in on those who concerned us while we were here."

"I wouldn't have expected that I concerned you so greatly, Cato," Prosper said, and the dead man grinned merrily in reply.

"Well, of course, you do, Mister Creale. After all, it was you who sent me there, so naturally, I am attentive to your affairs in the calm that followed that storm."

Prosper had been about to tell Cato that the days following his death had been anything but calm, but then the first rays of the dawn had tickled his nose and awoken him.

Drying his hands, Prosper shook his head to dismiss all the dreams, although he reminded himself that he must share the one about the kittens with Tace, if only to hear her shriek of delight at the thought. On further consideration, though, it might be best to only do so with his hat securely stored out of the reach of both kittens and small children.

His first errand of the morning was to return to town, where he wanted to consult with the magistrate regarding some of the questions that had plagued him as he tried to sleep. He was aware of the limits of his knowledge of such matters, as they had never applied to his needs before. Now that they were, he was loath to wait for answers.

On the outskirts of the village, he encountered Missus Grant, who was carrying a large basket laden with a variety of greenery and flowers. She greeted him with a broad smile.

"How does your family, Mister Creale? I trust they are in good health, and that you have had little use for the feverfew you last came to me for?"

He nodded. "Aye, little Tace made a full recovery, and my wife entirely credits your physicking for it."

She scoffed. "Oh, I did not perform any true physic, but only applied what any attentive student of nature might observe for herself of the valuable qualities of various diverse plants."

Prosper gestured his acquiescence with his hands. "As you say, yet she laughs and plays today, and for that I am grateful to you."

She gave him a shrewd look then. "I have heard a rumor that there are many on your plantation who have reason to be grateful to you. Is it true that you have freed your slaves from bondage?"

Prosper nodded, feeling suddenly hesitant to discuss the matter widely, especially as it was apparently already a subject of much conversation around the community. "Aye, I have," he said, without offering further explanation.

She closed her eyes and hugged her basket closely, as the

nearest thing to pure joy Prosper could recall her face reflecting passed over her. Opening her eyes, she said, "I give you joy of your delivery from the awful corruption of the spirit that arises from the belief that any man is good enough to own another. You have done your hands a great service, but also yourself."

Prosper was a bit taken aback at her words, and it took him a moment to reply, civilly, "Thank you kindly." He hesitated and then added, "I must confess that I did not come to this decision on my own, but acted under the direction of God to end the bondage of my fellow-creatures."

She shook her head dismissively. "Whatever moved you to the act, it was a righting of wrongs, and I am greatly pleased to hear you confirm it from your own mouth. These are strange times, and folks pass the most incredible rumors about, arising from misunderstandings and ill intentions."

"Truer words have rarely been spoken, friend." Prosper realized that her approval was a balm for the hurt he'd felt at the overheard comments yesterday. "As it happens, I am on my way to learn whether I can more completely right the wrongs of having taken by force the labor of my former slaves. I intend to offer each of them a grant of some of my disused land, to enable them to make some sort of living upon it."

Missus Grant looked startled, and then said, slowly, "I cannot see any reason that you should not be able to do so, and it is a gracious thing to contemplate doing."

Prosper shook his head, frowning. "Nay, it is only the merest approach to grace, and some might even say that I mean it more to salve my own guilt for what I have done to them over the years than to improve their situation. Still, it is what I can contemplate doing under the present circumstances, so long as the law will permit the hands to receive property from me and own it."

Missus Grant pursed her lips thoughtfully. "I do not see why they should not be able to receive property. Why, I know of a free negro up in Baltimore County who not only owns land, but who even votes, so great are his property holdings."

"Do you, now? That is excellent news, and answers the question that I came to town to inquire about."

"I encountered the man in the course of my travels — this was when it was safe to travel even great distances to seek the ingredients for my medicines — and he impressed me greatly, as being not only well educated, but dedicated to his inquiries into both the natural world, and that of men, as well."

She got a distant look in her eyes, a smile crossing her face at the memory of the encounter. "Terribly clever, too. He told me of a clock that he constructed after having examined a pocket watch, and was delighted with the fact that it kept good time even after several years, and struck the hour right along with the bells of the church."

Prosper's eyebrows rose. "A prodigious accomplishment for any man, I warrant. He must be a creature of some most impressive parts, and I find that I am envious of you for the chance to have to met him."

She shrugged. "As I said, it was some years ago. It impressed upon me the absurdity of the arguments that some men were best suited to manual labor, while others were meant to be their masters. I came away from my interview with Mister Banneker firmly convinced that any man, given adequate opportunity, could rise to a level of accomplishment that would have little to do with his original station in life."

"A provocative and radical insight, and one which I will strive to take to heart. I fear that I still under-estimate the capacities of the men I have held for so long."

"Habits of many years do not disappear overnight, Mister Creale. You are to be commended for undertaking the effort, and ought to give yourself grace for those moments when you realize that you have fallen short of your intentions."

He nodded gravely. "I shall endeavor to follow your sage advice, and with the information which you have shared with me, I can return home and attempt to put it into practice."

He bowed to her in farewell and turned to go. She called after him, halting him in his tracks. "Do not forget to attend to the needs of your family, as you attend to the needs of your conscience."

Prosper turned and offered her a rueful smile. "Once again, you pierce to the heart of the matter in just a few words. I am grateful, and will remember what you've said."

Chapter 15

Prosper was making further adjustments to the plow when Clement found his father in the barn. The plow had still not been as rigid as Prosper would have liked, and he was trying various shims and wedges to bring it back to the same level of ruggedness as the original.

Without preamble, Clement blurted, "Father, is it true that you mean to further diminish your legacy by not only disposing of your slaves to manumission, but much of your land holdings, as well?"

Prosper took his time, tapping in a wedge with gentle hammer blows before he straightened up and answered. "I am not acting with the purpose of diminishing the legacy that I will someday" — he put a deliberate stress on the word — "leave to you children, but with the intent that my legacy, whatever its size, will not be one of sin and suffering."

Clement's eyes narrowed. "Is Godliness only to be found in poverty, then?"

"Certainly not!" Mastering the flash of anger that had heated his reply, Prosper continued more calmly. "The blessed Lord does not mean for us to suffer, but neither will He overlook us committing the gravest of sins in order to enjoy earthly wealth. It was for this reason that He said that it is easier for a camel to go through the eye of a needle, than for a rich man to enter into His kingdom."

Clement scowled. "Whatever God has to say in the matter, you can hardly deny that your actions of the past several days have left your children with much less to hope for from you. I heard the twins whispering to each other, concerned about whether you will be able to offer any sort of meaningful dowry at all for either of them, when the time comes."

"Well, for one thing, that time is nowhere near, and for another, these are uncertain days in every regard. Nothing is promised to any of us, no matter how much we might wish it so. I should like very much to stand before you and say with utter certainty that you and your brothers will be each granted a fine plantation, and that your sisters will have generous settlements when they find husbands."

He looked out of the barn toward the eastern horizon. "There are many things I would like to be able to be certain of, but that is not the way of the world, nor has it ever been." He glanced back at Clement. "The only thing that I am certain of is that there will come a day when we each must meet our Maker, and I do not intend to stand before Him and say that I heard His warning, but chose to ignore it."

Clement gave him a sour look, and said, "There is the uncertainty of a world that is being turned upside-down by radical agitators, and then there is the certainty of actions by one man that seem to pursue a design to reduce us to beggars on what remains of our own land."

Prosper looked at the young man, a frown of disapproval coming over his own face in answer to the one he found on his son's. "You are dangerously close to showing me open disrespect, son. Whether or not you agree with my actions, I am owed that much as your father. We can disagree while still discussing it in a civil manner, but you must not forget yourself in your frustration with me."

Clement again pursed his mouth sourly, but he said only, "Yes, Father. I meant no disrespect. I will only ask this, in all humble politeness: Do not forget your duties to your family as you weigh your duties to God. As I believe you have taught us, the Lord is forgiving of all things that one must do in order to be able to glorify His name."

"The Lord will forgive sins made in error or innocence, but He has made it abundantly clear to me what is the least that I can do to end the sin I have committed in holding our fellow-creatures in bondage. My conscience has directed some of my actions, it is true, but I do not think that yours would permit you to do less, were you in my position. Conscience, too, has kept me mindful of the duties owed to you and the rest of my family."

He sighed. "Son, someday, you will need to wrestle with matters of at least as much import as these in your own life. I fervently hope that when that time comes, you will feel as certain as I do in choosing the path you must take." He did not add that he wished that he were as certain as he was trying to sound.

Clement frowned again, but this time, at least, there didn't seem to be so much judgment of his father's actions in it. "Father, can you at least tell me how much of the woods will be left in our name when you are finished?"

"More than I am granting to these men," Prosper said, with much more conviction. He had spent a long afternoon figuring out how many years each of the men he'd manumitted had served him, and matching that up against the amount of land that he held. It had come as no small relief when he'd discovered that even with Frankie's many years of service, and the lengthy service of some of the others as well, the compensation he'd contemplated would not dispose of even half of what his own father's legacy had been to him.

Clement seemed to relax considerably at this news. "I am happy to hear that, at least. The girls need not worry about the provisions for their settlements, in that case."

"Nor will you boys need to be concerned about having a sufficient legacy," Prosper confirmed. "I will not dissemble, though. I do not intend to provide you with a life of ease, but only to grant you the means by which you may make your living. This presumes, as well, that the Lord does not place more obstacles in our paths before the blessed day when he calls me home to his side."

Clement's mouth turned down in another scowl, but this one was of denial rather than anger. "I do not look for that day to come anytime soon, Father."

"I know you do not, son. But when it does, I hope to leave my earthly concerns in a state that will not trouble my mind in the hereafter." He gave Clement a quick smile, acknowledging the impiety of the comment.

His son hesitated visibly, and then blurted out a fresh question. "Tell me, what did the voice of God sound like?"

"Like a man whose voice was unfamiliar to me, speaking directly into my ear, but nowhere to be seen. There was no specifically Godly quality to it, though that was likely out of His desire to have me hear His word, rather than just His voice. Of course, I cannot speculate as to the workings of the Lord's mind."

He smiled again, and Clement smiled back, his earlier anger clearly dissipated now.

Prosper motioned to the plow. "I need to finish up this work before dinner time, all right?"

The young man nodded and turned to leave, then turned back. "Father?"

"Yes, son?"

"I apologize for any offense I may have given you in my confusion and worry. I ought to have granted you the benefit of trusting that you would act in our best interests, as you answered the call of the Lord's word."

Prosper acknowledged the apology with a bow of his head. "The blessed Lord is not always an easy master to serve, but He always directs our actions to our own best interests. As a father and as the head of the household, I seek to emulate our heavenly Father in this regard, even when I must ask difficult things of you all."

Clement nodded. "I shall endeavor to remember that, Father, and I appreciate your efforts on our behalf."

After his son had departed, Prosper thought over the exchange as he finished making the adjustments to the plow. The fact that Clement had felt he needed to come and confront him troubled Prosper, and he felt a moment of guilt for having failed to share with the rest of the family the scope of his wealth even after the changes that the Lord had demanded of him.

He had to confess, too, that his resolution of the practical implications of the commands of his conscience — inspired by God or of his own will — had come as a relief. While he did not feel the sudden freedom of spirit that Mister Garrettson had testified to having experienced, he did feel a sense of general relief now that he had settled the matter.

The former slaves had been, variously, unsure what to make of his offer of compensation for their past compulsory service, overjoyed at the opportunity it represented, or filled with further questions. Some of these questions had been easy to answer — could they truly hold land? — and others would require more thought before he could give them an adequate answer. Cain had asked whether they would be responsible for working the land themselves, or whether they might rely on Prosper to help.

In truth, he felt that he had discharged his entire responsibility for the sins of the past by granting them the unimproved land, and that they ought to accept it without demanding yet more of him, but he could see, too, that being turned out onto a wooded plot with no tools or assistance from other men was a daunting prospect, particularly for someone whose background prepared them only for the management of land already converted to agricultural purposes.

Perhaps he could offer them the use of some tools, on a loan basis, or perhaps he could even fairly ask them to lease tools from him, at reasonable rates. In any event, the question of how they could best make use of the land they were granted was one that countless generations of men had found answers to in the past, and Prosper felt certain that such active and capable men as these would do likewise, with or without his help.

He had just finished up with the plow, and was on his way back to the house when he spied a horse and rider flying along the road up to his plantation. He rarely got visitors on horseback, never mind one that was in this much of a hurry, so he stood and waited for the man's arrival.

When the rider pulled his horse to a stop, Prosper noted that the animal was in a lather, telling him that the rider had driven him hard, for an extended period. Breathless, the man announced, "The British have been sighted entering the bay of the Chesapeake, and every man is called upon to do his duty in providing for the defense of the state."

Prosper's eyebrows rose. There had been prior alarms regarding British incursions into the bay, and there was the ever-present potential that they would use its natural access to the vicinity of Philadelphia to attempt a sudden strike aimed at the Congress there. None had come with this level of alarm, though, and he asked, gravely, "What specific actions are we to take in answer to this challenge?"

"In the present moment, you are to ensure that you are armed at all times, and alert to the enemy's appearance along our roads. Where they have traveled elsewhere in the countryside, they have left in their wake a trail of ruined farms and ravaged people. You cannot suffer them to pass without every possible resistance."

Prosper nodded. He had enough worries about the security of his plantation's financial future without the additional prospect of a passing marauding army undoing the delicate balance he had struck.

"In addition, if you have not yet given thought to service in the Continental Army, the need is ever-present there. They need men of unwavering commitment to the independence of America, and with a range of experience."

From behind himself, Prosper heard Clement's voice, and realized that his son had come to see what the fuss was, even as the words that the young man spoke sank in.

"I will volunteer for the Continentals. With whom do I speak?"

Chapter 16

At the dinner table, Prosper was enduring a furious silence from Kristine, and this time, it wasn't even because of something that he had done. She was past even acknowledging Clement's presence at the table, but her husband unhappily had her full attention.

Finally, she spoke, her words bitterly spat from between clenched teeth. "Could you do nothing to stop our son from throwing his life into the mercies of General Washington's army, husband?"

Prosper looked at her helplessly. "He is of an age to take such decisions without my consent, wife, as you know well. And it may have come to your attention that he is possessed of a strong will, the inheritance of a parent likewise endowed."

Her expression grew downright dangerous now, and Phillip began to whimper, even though she had said nothing to him. She retorted, "Do I take you to mean that you are trying to hold me responsible for our son's nature?"

He grimaced tolerantly. "Do you think me unaware of my own faults in having a stubborn habit of mind?"

She softened not at all, shooting back, "You are the one making all the changes of late, while I am left to make do as well as I can with a household whose means are diminished by your actions, and where our prospects for future improvement are darker with every passing day."

Prosper blinked rapidly, then tried to rally. "I did not know that it was such a struggle, wife. Your allowance for our household expenses has not been reduced by one shilling, though our income for the year's harvest will not be known for some months yet."

"Nay, the allowance has not changed, though all the prices in the markets certainly have, so that what once served to permit me to bring a satisfying variety of dishes to the table now is scarcely enough to enable a meager minimum. Had you not noticed that where once I served meat, I have been reduced to beans on a regular basis? Or does the effort I put into providing you with your daily sustenance go unnoticed in your fervor for new philosophies?"

Prosper felt a flush of anger fall over himself as he absorbed her words, and it seemed that she detected the sudden shift in him, and realized that she had gone too far in her criticism. She said, hurriedly, "It is your right, of course, to adopt what philosophies as may seem fit to you, and it is my duty to support you as you do so."

Coldly, he said, "If this is how you express your support, I should shudder to think what form your opposition might take. You are possessed of a sharp tongue, but you ought also be possessed of enough wisdom to know when you ought to hold that tongue, and under what circumstances you may give it leave to lash those around you. This is not one of those circumstances, wife."

"Yes, husband," she said, her contrition sounding genuine enough. But Prosper knew, too, that her anger was also quite real, and he considered her as the children looked on, wide-eyed in their surprise at seeing their parents argue openly in front of them.

Finally, Prosper said, his tone softening just a touch, "If your household allowance is no longer sufficient, you need only inform me of that fact, and we can discuss together what adjustments might we need to make to permit you to set the table you believe is appropriate."

She said, stiffly, but without the heat of her earlier tone, "I should like that, as soon as you have a moment to spare. I know you do not eat for the purpose of relishing the fine things that Providence may set on your table, but only to strengthen yourself to serve God. I should not be judgmental toward you for that, but should celebrate the fact that you are so dedicated to the purpose for which you were placed upon this Earth."

"We shall discuss it later this evening, then, after you have the children put to bed. And, for my part, I am sorry that I do not often enough pause to appreciate the skill with which you serve our table. I know that you take pride in it, and I should give you the praise that you earn from it."

Kristine said nothing, but he could tell by the way that her shoulders relaxed just a tiny, barely perceptible degree that she was pleased with his comments. Peering into the bowl before him, he asked, "What have you prepared for us today?"

She waved her hand in a dismissive gesture. "Just a plain soup of an old chicken, hardly worth taking note of."

He gave her a frown, and she shrugged, adding, "It is enough to keep body and soul together, and more than that is hardly necessary in these days when there is so little to celebrate."

With a scowl, she turned now to Clement. "Indeed, there is nothing whatever to celebrate today, save for the cold knowledge that my eldest child cares more for the idea of being shot at by redcoats than he does for the comfort of his mother."

Clement protested, "But, Mother, the British have

committed every form of depravity against our people, from the denial of the most cherished of our rights to the wanton destruction of our neighbors' very lives. As a man of conscience, I had no choice but to stand up in the defense of our nation."

"This rebellion does not merit the declaration of a new nation," Kristine snapped. "We may have sympathy for the cause of freedom, and even harbor a belief that the independence of these colonies may one day come about as a natural consequence of history, without throwing away our lives in a vain attempt to bring it about before its time."

Clement shook his head violently. "Mother, if all men behaved as you propose, nothing would ever be accomplished in the progress of mankind toward a better state. Boldness is its own reward, and independence is but the consequence of liberty. If there were a way to achieve liberty without striking for independence, why, I should be all for it. As it stands, however, the despot on the throne in England has left no doubt about his intent to rule us with a fist of iron. Well, then, we shall have to answer with iron ourselves."

He glared at his mother with a defiant jut of his chin, and she seemed ready to answer when Prosper spoke mildly, trying to mollify both of them. "The way to improvement of the state of humanity is through seeking to emulate our Lord and Savior. Recall that He was not one to tolerate temporal authority when it was abusive of its prerogatives, and yet in the end, He submitted to the will of Pontius Pilate, and did not call upon His disciples to resist."

Prosper placed his hands flat on the tabletop for emphasis. "Wife, there is no use in berating our son; he has made his commitment, and whether or not we agree with it, he is a man and able to chart the course of his own life. If it is the will of God that he shall be returned to us unhurt, we shall celebrate that in due time. If the Lord in His infinite wisdom and mercy has some other plan for Clement, then we cannot protest against Him."

Looking sterner now, he took in his entire family with a glance around the table. "If this is to be the last meal that we enjoy together, let us do so in harmony, and with the kindness that we each owe to one another."

Kristine grimaced, but said nothing further, while Clement returned to eating, a mulish expression on his face. Prosper shook his head, but kept his counsel, knowing well enough that it was likely that this was the best he could hope for from the two of them.

After the meal, Prosper rose and returned to the fields to check on the work that the hands were performing there. While most of them had responded to the offer of their own land with enthusiasm and even joy, leaping to do their duties with a greater alacrity than ever before, a couple of the younger men still required close supervision. Primus was not yet comfortable enough in his role to instruct them when they needed instruction, so it fell to Prosper to do so.

Jack was particularly likely to misinterpret his tasks — though always in the favor of the least effort, which made it seem unlikely to be mere stupidity — and so Prosper approached him where he was bent at the task of plucking pests from the young corn stalks.

At this point in the season, the worms were just starting to give over to the grasshoppers in doing damage to the young leaves and shoots, and Prosper frowned to see how many of the stalks were showing the signs of having been attacked under the ground, with withered leaves and twisted shoots.

There was little that anyone could do about worms underground, he knew, but it did nothing for his mood to find Jack doing little more than desultorily making his way down the row, ruffling the leaves of the plants as he went. This action would roust out the grasshoppers, but leave them alive to return moments later to continue their work of chewing down the leaves.

Prosper called out, "Ho, there, Jack." The young man startled at his voice, having evidently not seen his approach.

"Oh, Mister Creale, I thought you were still at your dinner."

Prosper frowned slightly at the man's near-confession that he had been taking the easy way out of his work, and said, irritably, "Unlike some, I knew that there was work to be done. Listen to me — if you but send the grasshoppers away, and suffer them to live, they will fly back to their meal as soon as you have passed. You must not fail to catch and destroy them, as I've shown you."

Jack shuddered visibly. "I just so dislike the feeling of their insides on my fingers, Mister Creale. If I disturb them often enough from their meal of corn, I expect that they will move on to some easier meal in time." Prosper noted that the man was unapologetic about the ineffectiveness of his approach.

"You could drop them into a bucket of water," Prosper said, an edge of anger in his voice. "Or stuff them into a bag, which you could throw upon a fire later. Even with you raising a ruckus among them, there is nothing else that they love to eat so much as my corn, once they have discovered it. They must depart this earth for all time, lest they leave us with nothing come the harvest."

"I suppose that I understand what is at stake well enough. I hadn't thought of using a bag," the young man said, his face twisted in uncertainty. "But have you any to spare for such a purpose?"

"I am certain that you could fashion one tonight from some old clothing, if you applied yourself," Prosper said, trying to keep the irritation out of his tone. "In the meantime, a bucket will work well enough. Or you can do it the easy way, and just clean your hands afterward."

Jack shuddered again, his eyelids fluttering with distaste. "I will fetch a bucket and water," he said, and hurried off, grumbling under his breath.

While he waited for the field hand's return, Prosper took out his irritation on the insects he could find on a row of corn, feeling a tiny kernel of satisfaction with the pop of each one's torso as he dispatched them.

Though they were tiny, by working in concert with thousands of their fellows, they could cost him so much of his harvest as to upset the ever-more precarious balance between ruin and survival at the end of the growing season. Each one that he left crushed in the soil brought him that much closer to being able to live up to his name.

He was still reflecting on the effectiveness of a mass of small individuals against the efforts of one man when Primus came out from behind the barn, looking agitated. He made his way across the field toward Prosper, stepping carefully, but hurriedly, over the rows.

Primus arrived a bit out of breath, and announced, "Jack done told me that you checked him for not properly doing his work. He was pretty mightily worked up by the time I saw him and said that he didn't think he wanted to work here any longer. Last I saw of him, he was headed off to his plot in the woods."

Prosper said nothing at first, but sighed and shook his head, returning to the work that the young field hand had so precipitously abandoned. Finally, he stood and faced the foreman. "How am I to manage a plantation when men can just up and leave whenever the fancy strikes them? Is there no way that you can prevail upon him to return to his job?"

Primus frowned, considering his answer. Finally, he said, "I believe that if you were to offer Jack an apology for speaking to him sharp, he might come on back. But you'll need to go to his plot, as I do not think that he will answer your summons."

Prosper took a deep breath, willing the rage that had suddenly welled within him to come under control. The cheek of these men, to whom he had given so much, in insisting that he treat them as if they were . . .

His shoulders slumped, as a voice — probably his own inner voice this time — supplied the rest of the thought. "As if they were equals, which is what you told them they are." The habits of a lifetime of holding other men in bondage were going to take more than a piece of paper to break, he realized.

Resignedly, he said, "Very well. I will go to him. Thank you, Mister Primus."

Chapter 17

The corn was hip-high, and Prosper could see Jack moving among the stalks, stooping to pull bugs off the leaves, carefully tucking each one into a bag he had tied to his belt. The man seemed cheerful, and Prosper wished that his own mood was as bright.

After giving Kristine her increased allowance for the month's household expenses, the purse he kept in his money-hole was nearly empty, and the harvest was still some endless months off. He was going to need to either ask the merchants in town for credit, or else sell off something of substantial value in order to get to that day.

Having already disposed of so much of the woods that had been his legacy from his father, he was loath to sell more of the fallow land, but he could see little choice. Debt was even more unappealing, and carried with it the very real risk he would wind up in prison for failure to satisfy the agreements he'd made, if any unanticipated event overcame his little operation.

Already, a fierce spring thunderstorm had torn away the topsoil holding the roots in place along rows of the lower section of the field, and Prosper had spent a long, anxious day leading a team of hands through the delicate operation of shoring up the corn stalks that were loosened by the running water.

At least the storm had soaked the field for the day. A long stretch of sunny, dry days, lovely to behold, but leaving the young corn drooping in its rows, had required that the men be employed in bringing water by hand up from the creek, bucket after laborious bucket, to carefully pour over the roots of the plants. After a fortnight of repeating this back-breaking exercise, Prosper had heard one of the hands whisper angrily to his neighbor, "Perhaps we ought to just let God's will be done, and leave this field to die."

Prosper had whirled to see who had spoken, but everyone he saw gave every appearance of being diligently bent to their tasks, so he let the comment pass unchallenged. He resolved on the spot, though, to attend to the education of his men at the earliest opportunity. Sunday could not come soon enough.

He arose early on the Sabbath, as was his habit anyway, but with a fresh sense of purpose this time. After breaking fast with Kristine and the children, he went out to the former slave quarters with his Bible in his hand. Although some of the men had begun constructing themselves cabins on their plots in the woods, most still gathered at their old quarters for meals, and Prosper seated himself on an upturned log and waited for them all to arrive for their breakfast.

He greeted each man by name, warmly and with respect, but with such a grave expression on his face that several of them asked whether something was amiss. He assured them that all was well, but said nothing further to allay their fears.

Eventually, only a few were absent, and he stood up and began. "Men, I have been remiss in regularly offering you the good news of our Savior's sacrifice and forgiveness, and I mean to correct this oversight immediately. I am no preacher, but I will do my best to share the word of God with you."

The men gathered before him, most looking attentive,

though Prosper thought he caught an eye roll shared between two of the younger men. He ignored it, though, and opened his Bible.

"In the Gospel of Matthew, our blessed Savior tells us to pray, saying 'Thy will be done in earth, as it is in heaven,' but does not give us any direct instruction as to what form His will might take. If you are confused by God's will, take heart from the knowledge that you are not alone in this, but let me offer some thoughts to help guide your pursuit of the truth of His will."

Even the younger men were paying attention, which Prosper was gratified to see. Pleased at having found a topic that would speak to their curiosity, he continued. "God's will can be found in three different regions of our experience of Him. The first is His secret will, which He does not choose to share with us as He directs the workings of the world. These are the things that do not concern our daily lives, but which figure into His plan for the whole world."

"We must trust in these mysteries to lead to our redemption from sin and our deliverance to the blessed salvation of our souls, without expecting to know the details — nor even to understand those details — if they were to come to our knowledge. Our God is mighty and, in His nature, He is beyond our comprehension on Earth."

Primus' eyes narrowed ever so slightly in skepticism, but Prosper felt confident that the rest of his sermon would explain his meaning clearly to even the most unwilling listener, so he continued. "Next is our discernment of His will, which we may discover in the decisions that the blessed Lord's spirit leads us to daily, whether or not we are aware of His guidance. Those choices we make we can see are good and right are those to which He has led us, and it is in the goodness of the outcomes of those choices that we can find the will of God."

Prosper closed his Bible now, warming to the subject. "When a friendship struck up between men bears fruit in their mutual regard, in the business that they may conduct together, in their freedom to share confidences between them, they have both correctly discerned God's will, and He is rewarding them for doing so."

He could see that point hit its mark by the expressions on several of the men's faces, and so he continued. "When we see a man who is successful in his pursuits, whose every action seems as though it is blessed by God, that is because it is blessed by the Lord, because that man has acted in accordance with God's will."

He gestured toward the woods, which were largely owned now by the men who sat before him. "When I granted you each land from my former holdings, I was, I believe, acting according to my discernment of God's will. In the fullness of time, we shall see whether God smiles upon that decision, but I feel quite confident in the rectitude of my act."

Several of the men involuntarily smiled when he mentioned the possibility of God's smile, and Prosper smiled in turn. "Finally, there is God's revealed will, and this is both the most direct and the most unusual way for God to make His will known to man. When I chose to give you all your freedom from bondage, it was because God spoke to me to remind me that I had been granted much, and as a consequence, much was expected of me."

He saw several of the men shift about uncomfortably. He had not shared his experience with anyone but Kristine until now, and he wondered whether they doubted his sanity as much as he initially had himself. "Even more unambiguous was God's word to my friend Mister Garrettson, whom God told plainly that he must release his slaves from bondage. I took this direction to heart and came home and began writing out your manumissions."

He looked around at the men and found that their expressions were much more open and accepting than they had had been at the start of this last leg of the sermon. "One acts against the revealed will of God at one's own peril, for to ignore it is to openly declare one's allegiance to the devil, and the devil will take your soul for all eternity once you have done that."

He shook his head sadly. "I should not wish that fate upon any of you, so it is crucial that you each should try in your every deed to act in accordance with the will of God, whether that will be secret, discerned, or revealed. We should not merely guess at God's will, or suppose that we will know it naturally, but we should pray constantly that He will reveal it to us, and that He may see fit to guide our actions to embody fully His will. And, if He does not, well, we should remain satisfied that He has a plan for our salvation."

Bowing his head, he said, "My brothers in Christ, let us pray." A few of the men bowed their heads immediately, but the rest followed suit within a few moments, and he began.

"Dear Lord, I pray that Thou wilt lift the sin from each of our hearts, and that Thou wilt guide us each to Thy holy light, and that Thou wilt show each of us where our duty to Thee lies. We labor together to glorify Thy name, and pray that Thou wilt show us the way as we do so. I thank Thee for Thy endless blessings, and for the salvation that Thou dost offer to each of us. I pray, also, for the fruitful bounty of a harvest that will sustain us through these times of trial, and will permit us to leave our earthly cares behind with a joyful heart when that blessed day comes that Thou dost decide to call Thy faithful servants home. These things I pray of Thee, in the blessed name of our Lord, Amen."

Prosper heard a murmured "Amen" in response, and looked up to find that his men were looking back at him as though with a single mind. Despite himself, he smiled. "Let us enter the new week of work together with the sole purpose of discovering what God's will is for us, all right?"

"Yes, sir," said Primus. "And I give thanks, as well, that God has given us a friend such as you, who is willing to share His word with us, despite the difference in our stations in this life."

Prosper scoffed, "The blessed Lord does not see the differences between us, but sees only the yearning within each of our souls to follow Him and to glorify His name together. I feel completely confident of having discerned His will in this matter." He smiled, and Primus returned the smile.

Turning to leave, he called out to the group, "May God bless and keep each one of you today, and may He guide your steps in the week ahead. Enjoy the remainder of your day of rest and reflection."

Walking back up toward the house, Prosper realized that he felt truly at peace for the first time in many weeks, and he wished only that he might have taken the time before this to share the Gospel with his field hands. He shook his head to dispel the moment of regret, wanting to enjoy the serenity that infused his being for a few moments more before he returned to Kristine's company.

Ever since Clement's departure to join what had recently been designated as the First Maryland Regiment, Kristine's mood had oscillated between joy at receiving one of his regular letters, and despairing terror during the wait for the next one. As it had been over a week since the last post from him, she had been growing increasingly anxious for the past few days. He would have to remind her that the post did not normally move on the Sabbath, and that they could not expect a delivery today, in any event.

His own retreat to prayer on the behalf of his son's safety was troubled by the most recent evening meeting with Mister Garrettson's now reduced congregation. The man had been in rare form that night, though his voice was hoarse, which cut his sermon short. For all of its brevity, though, it lacked none of his characteristic punch.

"It is said that in some of these colonies, there have been circulated demands that all men should swear oaths of loyalty to the individual governments being established on these shores in the wake of the independence."

He shook his head, an expression of firm resolve on his face. "To begin with, I do not hold with the swearing of oaths in the Lord's holy name, and even less do I agree with demanding that men swear loyalty to any body but their Maker."

He glanced around the room, as though looking for rebel spies, and then said quietly, the hoarseness in his voice more audible, "Indeed, until this matter is concluded on the field of battle, I should not like to see any man held to break with our duty to the King as members of his church on Earth."

"I know, I know," he said, holding up his hands to quiet the confused murmuring that arose from the congregation. "The question of our affiliation with the Church of England is a matter of some controversy, as with so many things in these days of strife and division. The rector at Chaptico Church has altered their book of Common Prayer to refer no longer to the King, but instead prays for the Lord to grant wisdom and discernment to the Congress."

He frowned, looking as though he'd bitten into something sour. "While we are not bound by these alterations, they are meant to guide our practices here in the countryside, as well as within the churches themselves. And then, there is the matter of their opposition to the will of God, as revealed to me, that none of us should hold in bondage our fellow-creatures. If the devil has their ear in this matter, how are we to trust that they are not following his lead in the whole of their rebellion?"

He sighed. "I do not know where the truth of the matter lies, but I cannot escape the suspicion that the entire enterprise is another trick of Satan to lead our dear Savior's flock astray. I would only warn each of you to avoid any open declaration for either side, if you possibly can. If your position in the earthly affairs of your community demands it, and your own conscience can bear it, you can, of course, sign any loyal oaths that they ask of you, but you must not take up arms."

Again, the congregation stirred uneasily, and again, Mister Garrettson raised his hands to silence them. "From reading, from my own reflections, and from the teachings of the good Spirit, I am drawn quite away from a belief in the lawfulness of the shedding of human blood, even under the dispensation offered in the Gospels in the most extreme case where it is in the defense of our own lives. I am not persuaded in any event that we have reached that point in our contest with the mother country."

He looked around, and repeated with emphasis, "We cannot in good conscience support those who fight for the independence of these colonies from the Crown."

Chapter 18

With the preacher's declaration running through his head, Prosper had struggled at first with how to respond to Clement's letters. With the love due to a son from his father, certainly, but could he offer the young man encouragement in his convictions when Mister Garrett's suspicions remained in the air?

So, he wrote to Clement of the duty owed to the Lord, and reminded him to attend to his prayers and to keep the Sabbath as strictly as he could. He shared what news there might be of events on the plantation, though he avoided sharing events concerning the former slaves, out of a desire to avoid stirring up resentment in the young man's heart against the actions he had found necessary.

He felt certain that Clement would have been most interested in the progress that Cain had made, joining his plot together with Frankie's exceptionally large one, and building a generously proportioned cabin on it for the two of them to share. Prosper wasn't sure what surprised him more — Cain's sweet devotion to the older man's comfort, or his skill at executing a complex and rugged design for their residence.

The plan for Frankie to travel to see his brother seemed to have been set aside for the time being. None of the men wanted to discuss it, but it was apparent that the small group that had set out from the plantation with their freshly inked manumissions had encountered some sort of a terrible event before they had turned back to plead for a place to stay until they could decide upon a new course of action.

The land grants Prosper had given each of them had offered them a more viable option than a life on the margins of society, trying to find work while having no permanent residence or savings to fall back upon. Prosper felt a sense of satisfaction at having arrived at a solution that worked better for them than simply turning them out once their service to him was at an end.

Clement had long relied upon Cain to help him execute his various schemes for diversion in the woods or around the plantation, and Prosper was certain that under different circumstances, his son would have taken an equal measure of satisfaction at seeing his old companion thriving so. But the fact that he saw Cain's good fortune as having come at the expense of his own eventual inheritance spoiled any pleasure that Clement might have otherwise felt, and so Prosper left it out of his letters.

Instead, he gave Clement updates on the progress of his sisters and brothers, news of the kittens' exploits, and brief descriptions of the progress of the crop. He always closed by reminding Clement that he prayed daily for his son's safety and good health, and hoped that his son remembered his family in his own prayers.

Kristine sometimes gave him letters to include with his replies, her graceful looping handwriting a marked contrast to his own crabbed, heavy hand. Prosper did not read her missives, both out of respect for the privacy of his wife's thoughts, and because her way of expressing herself always made him irritable. As lovely as her hand was, her inability to commit thoughts to a page in a way that made any sense to him drove him mad when he had read from it.

Instead, he simply folded her letters into his own, and handed them over to the post rider, along with the money to pay for their passage to Clement. Always more money going out, and months yet until any more came in from the harvest.

As he reached the house, his buoyant mood from having shared the Gospel with the hands had evaporated at these solemn considerations, and he came to a decision. There was no more time to wait, watching his purse grow ever lighter.

He took a deep breath and entered the house, braced for whatever awaited him within. Sabbath mornings were often trying for the younger children, and as often as not, they would exasperate Kristine to the point of red-faced shouting. He felt a flash of guilt at having left her alone to deal with them, but reminded himself that it had been in the service of a worthy cause.

Instead of the angry chaos he had been prepared to face, he found quiet Sabbath studies underway in the sitting room. Kristine was reading to the younger children from her own copy of the Bible, and Prosper had to assume that it was one of the more engrossing passages, as they were paying rapt attention, instead of trying to escape her.

The twins and Humility were bent over a copy of the hymnal Prosper had purchased just the prior year, taking turns reading the verses in it. None of them knew the melodies to which the hymns were meant to be sung, so they instead were reciting them in a rhythmical chant.

Faith started a new hymn, intoning solemnly.

"To thee, most holy, and most high,

To thee, we bring our thankful praise;

Thy works declare thy name is nigh,
Thy works of wonder and of grace."

Hope picked up the next verse, her high, clear voice carrying across the room.

"Britain was doomed to be a slave,
Her frame dissolved, her fears were great;
When God a new supporter gave,
To bear the pillars of the state."

The book passed from one set of hands to the next, and Humility's deeper voice carried on.

"He from thy hand received his crown,
And swear to rule by wholesome laws,
His foot shall tread the oppressor down,
His arm defend the righteous cause."

They continued each in turn, and as he listened to the words of the hymn, Prosper frowned at the sentiment they reflected. Humility's turn came around again, and he chanted.

"No vain pretense to royal birth
Shall fix a tyrant on the throne:
God the great sovereign of the earth,
Will rise and make his justice known."

Prosper stepped forward. "Here, children," he said, "Let us select a different hymn, as this one seems rather too charged with the disorders of the world today."

Humility handed him the book, and Prosper paged through it, until he found one that seemed less likely to be quite as resonant with the political situation. He held the book open and handed it back to the boy. "Here, I like this one particularly well."

Humility nodded, and began reading.

"Lord of the worlds above,
How pleasant and how fair
The dwellings of thy love,
Thy earthly temples are!
To thine abode
My heart aspires,
With warm desires
To see my God."

Handing the book on to Faith, his finger marking the point where she should pick up, Humility glanced up to seek his father's approval, and Prosper smiled encouragement as his sister continued the hymn.

"The sparrow, for her young,
With pleasure seeks her nest;
And wandering swallows long
To find their wonted rest:
My spirit faints
With equal zeal
To rise and dwell
Among thy saints."

Hope then chanted the penultimate verse of the first part, before handing the book back to Humility, who finished the final verse before the annotated pause.

"They go from strength to strength,
Through this dark vale of tears,
Till each arrives at length,
Till each in heaven appears:
O glorious seat,
When God our king

Shall thither bring
Our willing feet!"

Prosper smiled at them, and nodded encouragement for them to finish with the second part of the hymn while he turned to Kristine. She glanced up as he approached the semicircle of the younger children arrayed before him but did not pause in her reading.

"And the waters prevailed, and were increased greatly upon the earth; and the ark went upon the face of the waters. And the waters prevailed exceedingly upon the earth; and all the high hills, that were under the whole heaven, were covered."

Prosper smiled even more broadly. It was little wonder that the children were listening with such close attention. The story of the Flood and of the Ark had always fascinated him when his father had read it. It helped that the otherwise solemn man had always broken away from the text of the Bible to enumerate the difficulties that Noah must have endured, trying to keep the lions away from the hares, and the flies from harassing everyone to the point of eliminating them.

Kristine opted for a more austere straight reading of the word of God, but the children were no less attentive for it. Nodding his approval to his wife, Prosper sat in his own chair and opened his copy of the Bible.

It fell open to the book of Job, and Prosper smiled grimly to himself. A more apt book he could scarcely imagine in his current circumstances. His eye fell upon Job's entreaty to God. "Remember, I beseech thee, that thou hast made me as the clay; and wilt thou bring me into dust again? Hast thou not poured me out as milk, and curdled me like cheese? Thou hast clothed me with skin and flesh, and hast fenced me with bones and sinews. Thou hast granted me life and favour, and thy visitation hath preserved my spirit."

Prosper indeed, felt as though he had been curdled like cheese this past year, and fenced in with bones and sinews from the pure life of the spirit which he so desired. Yet the blessed Lord had granted him life, and His visitation had done more than merely preserve his spirit.

Unlike Job, though, he did not feel the pull to the darkness of death, but only a taste of Job's weariness with the struggle of life. It was a struggle that he was still joyfully engaging with, though, and he let the book close, opening it again in the hopes of finding some happier passage upon which to ponder.

The third chapter of the book of Daniel lay before him, and he smiled at the clear parallels to the present moment. Did not the various governments who now contested control of the American colonies each have their own version of Nebuchadnezzar's golden statue to offer? Were they each not attempting to offer an idol that they demanded their subjects to dance before?

The fury of the king Nebuchadnezzar against his officials reminded Prosper both of King George's fury against those colonists who defied him, and of the rage unleashed by the most fervent of the Patriots against their Loyalist neighbors. And all, he reminded himself, would find their fate in the fiery furnace of God's judgment.

He took heart in the downfall of the old king's golden statue, as he read the familiar story, and nodded approvingly at the passage where the officials that the old king had attempted to consign to the pyre instead emerged from the flames unhurt.

The reminder that God would not tolerate the mockery by earthly authorities of His supremacy, and that those who attempted to use God for their own purposes would find only their downfall in doing so was particularly encouraging to Prosper's heart, and when he closed the Bible this time, he felt a sense of great reassurance.

The exploits of Nebuchadnezzar were doubtless incredibly disruptive to the people of his realm, but in the end, the Lord asserted his power over the power-mad king. So, who was the Nebuchadnezzar of this present age? Was it King George, upon his golden throne in distant London? Or was the old king's parallel to be found in the halls where the American Congress met, disrupting the previous order of the world for their own purposes?

Prosper sighed. In the end, he supposed, God would make His will clear, and like the field hands to whom he had just preached about the will of God, he would have to wait for the Lord to reveal what His plan was for these colonies.

In the meantime, he had worries enough in his earthly affairs, and needed to find a way to resolve them as quickly as possible. Once their day of prayer and consideration was concluded, it was time to tell Kristine how he planned to restore their financial security with the least possible additional damage to the wealth of their family.

Chapter 19

"As that strip of our property adjoins Mister Wrangell's, and we are not making any profitable use of it, it only makes sense to offer him favorable terms for it."

Prosper had laid out on the table the plan he'd sketched of his real property, back when he was marking out the plots that would be granted to each of his former slaves. Now he gestured to a section that lay on the other side of where the road up to the house bisected the upper field, and Kristine nodded, though not without a frown.

"If he is able to join that to his upper field, and eliminate the fence row that has divided them, he could increase the space allowed for his cattle to graze and could likely improve the size of his herd by nearly a dozen head."

Kristine objected, "If he takes out that fence row, the line of trees that gives the house shelter from the wind would go, as well, would it not?"

Prosper nodded. "Inevitably, yes, otherwise there would be little point in tearing down the fence itself. But if we plant new trees along the road to the house, they would form a natural frontier along our new property line, as well as a windbreak, in time."

"And in the meantime, we will be obliged to burn up more wood than ever to keep the house warm enough in the winter."

He raised a finger, smiling. "But once we cut those trees down, the wood they provide will supply us with what we need to make up for their loss as an interruption to the wind."

She shook her head at him, but said nothing, returning her attention to examining the plan minutely. "This will leave us with little more than the plot upon which the house and barn lie, in addition to the main field," she observed. "Can we even continue to call this a proper plantation with but one field?"

"We have for many years to this point, wife," he retorted, though he softened his words with a smile. "Nothing changes in our daily lives, in the house, or even in the output of our harvest, but this will make all the difference in being able to provide us with some certainty in these uncertain times."

"You presume that Mister Wrangell will be interested in buying the land from you."

"I have reason to believe that he will leap at the chance. He has often observed that we make little use of that strip, and that he would dearly love to expand upon his holdings, but that the good Lord is not making any new land upon which he might do so. Well, I have some perfectly fine old land, and it is time to make it produce a crop of guineas, since it is ill-suited to the golden corn."

Kristine rolled her eyes at his witticism, but waved a hand at him as he rose from the table, rolling up the plan. "No time like the present," he said, and tucked the rolled page under his arm. "I will be back shortly, hopefully with good news."

At Mister Wrangell's door, he hesitated before knocking. The cattle farmer was a bit old-fashioned, and might have preferred that Prosper send a note over first to arrange a meeting, but there were no hands he could spare to such a mundane task. He raised his hand and rapped sharply on the plain, red-painted door.

A young slave answered after a moment, her hair bound up under a colorful kerchief. Prosper gave her a minute bow and said, "Could you ask your master whether he is at liberty to receive a visit from Mister Creale, on a matter of business?"

"Certainly, sir," said the girl. "Should you like to come in and wait?"

Prosper bowed again, and she seemed a bit confused by the gesture as she held the door open for him, closing it as he entered the front hall of the house.

She had regained her aplomb as she told him, "You can sit there," indicating a long bench along one wall. "I will go and ask Mister Wrangell if he can receive you."

Prosper sat, considering the formality of how Wrangell ran his household. Where Kristine had always refused to consider house slaves, preferring to manage her own kitchen, Wrangell had nearly as large a staff in the house as out in the fields. Of course, he had owned fewer than Prosper had, since raising crops was necessarily more labor-intensive, but the other man's way of life was very different from his own.

In addition, he'd always needed to announce himself through the household staff, where Creale would usually answer his own door. Remembering the last meeting he'd had with Wrangell at his own door, Prosper found himself breaking out with beads of sweat on his lip. Perhaps this was a fool's errand, after all.

He took some steadying breaths, and reminded himself that no matter what political feeling might arise between them, this was a business matter of great advantage to the other man, and so there was no reason to think that he would refuse to consider the offer. Of course, to consider it, he would have to agree to hear it, so Prosper waited in nervous silence for the slave girl's return.

He heard her light steps approaching and rose to hear her answer. She stepped into the front hall and said, "Mister Wrangell is quite busy today, but he says that he can spare you a few minutes, if that will suit."

Prosper nodded agreeably. "I believe that we can discuss what I have to lay before him in that time, if he has more important matters to attend to."

The girl motioned to him. "Follow me, Mister Creale."

In the airy study, lit by tall windows that looked out over his fields, Mister Wrangell sat behind his desk, which was adorned with several neat stacks of papers and a couple of pamphlets and newspapers.

As Prosper entered the room, Wrangell stood to greet him. "Miss Katy tells me that you come on an errand of business, neighbor. Have you come to your senses and need to purchase some new field hands, or is it some other matter?"

Prosper stopped before the desk and gave the other man a respectful bow of his head, though he was raging inwardly at the snide comment. "Nay, sir, I come not to buy from you, but to see whether you might be interested in something I wish to sell."

Wrangell's eyebrows went up in what looked to Prosper like mock surprise, but he could see the other man glancing at the plan rolled up under his arm, and suspected that he knew immediately what was afoot. Still, he had to play his part in their little drama. He took the rolled page from beneath his arm and tapped it with his fingertip. "Have you a place where I can lay this out?"

"Certainly. Come over to this table with me, and I will

have Miss Katy clear away enough to make room." With a quick motion of his hand, he gestured to the slave girl, who swiftly moved to clear a space.

Prosper gave her a nod of gratitude and unrolled the paper upon the table. "You and I have discussed this strip along here a few times in the past, but I have always taken the position that I would find some profitable use to which I could put it." He tapped the long, thin strip of land represented on the page with a knuckle.

"I have concluded that it would be more sensible for me to offer you terms for this parcel, so that you can pursue the object that you have often mentioned of increasing the output of your farm."

Wrangell narrowed his eyes and leaned down to examine the plan, as though he had never heard the idea proposed before. He traced out the current boundary between their two properties, and then glanced out the window, which happened to offer a view of the tree line representing that same boundary.

"I will not deny that I have from time to time wondered at the odd configuration of your property, with plots on either side of the road to the house rendered nearly useless by their configuration." He shrugged theatrically. "It is not for me to judge how other men conduct their affairs, however, so I have left the matter alone."

Prosper mastered his urge to call the man a liar to his face, with the constant reference to how foolish his manumission of the slaves had seemed to him. Outwardly, he tilted his head in acknowledgment. "The property was so arranged when I inherited it, and I can only guess that when the plan for the house was made, it was the fashion to arrange the road to it in this manner."

With a gesture of his hands for emphasis, he said, "We are not in a time that permits the fashions of the past to lay a dead hand upon the tiller of our courses, however, and I believe firmly that it would be to our mutual benefit to move the boundary between our properties to lie against the easement for the road, for a reasonable consideration. In anticipation of that adjustment, I will remove the trees that mark the boundary, to save you the trouble. If you wish, I can even remove the fence, as well, and use its components to build a fence at the new boundary."

Wrangell made a dismissive gesture. "Those are details. Let us focus on the heart of the question. First, would it truly be to my benefit to annex this land from your holdings? If the answer to this question is clear enough, what would that annexation be worth to me, and can I make you a price that you can accept for it?"

"Of course," said Prosper, chiding himself for leaping ahead to the details that would have to wait until they had reached some sort of agreement to the initial sale. "Again, you have remarked at various times that you should like to increase your holdings. This offer presents an easy and natural means of doing so. Your cattle already graze up to the fence row" — and sometimes right through it, he did not add — "so expanding their range to incorporate this strip would be of little disruption to their habits."

Wrangell acknowledged the point with a small gesture, and Prosper went on. "As for price, this plot amounts to three and one-quarter acres, which would be turned over to you in a cleared state, ready for your use without needing further improvement." He tapped on the strip for emphasis. "This is prime land for your purposes, and you will not find its like at such a convenient placement at any other point in your lifetime."

The other man narrowed his eyes, as though expecting to be practiced upon by a sharp dealer. Instead, Prosper named a figure that was only a little more than the value of raw acreage at the frontiers of the colonies.

Wrangell's eyes widened in genuine surprise. "Why, Mister Creale, I had expected that you would try to take advantage of your position, but instead, you are willing to make me such terms as I would expect from a true friend!"

Prosper gave the man a look freighted with meaning before he replied, "That was my intent, sir. While you may not agree with my management of my plantation, I am still a friend to my neighbors, and, as I said when I entered, I believe that this arrangement will be to both our benefits."

Mister Wrangell offered Prosper his hand. "I was prepared to hear you ask a far higher price, and to talk you down to something more like what you've started at. I know that as a man of business, I should try to negotiate something more favorable to my own interests, but I cannot bring myself to do so at your expense."

Prosper accepted his neighbor's hand, relief washing over him in a nearly palpable wave. He could rely on staying out of debtor's prison, at least through the end of this growing season.

Chapter 20

Prosper was on one end of a great saw, borrowed from a lumberman in the village, and Primus was on the other, when the post rider came into view. He halloed and waved his arm at them as he approached, and so Prosper said to his workman, "Let us take the saw out for the moment, while I see what this fellow is about."

Primus nodded, and together, they worked the great saw out of the partial cut in the tree bordering Mister Wrangell's property. They carried the great blade to the cradle they had put together for it and set it down, careful not to let it flex too much.

Prosper pulled off his gloves and set them atop the handle, saying, "I'll be back as soon as possible. While you're waiting, perhaps you can pile up some of the brush." He gestured to the tangled limbs they had hewn from the trees that they had felled earlier in the morning.

"Yes, sir," Primus said, and moved to start gathering up some of the smaller branches, bundling them in his hands to drag over to the bonfire they would light when they were finished with the job.

Prosper met the horseman at the top of the road to the house, where the man handed him three letters. One was in Clement's familiar hand, but two others were in unknown handwriting, and Prosper frowned at the sight. He thanked the post rider and started toward the house, turning the unfamiliar letters over in his hands as he walked.

Inside, he went to his desk and broke open the seal on the first of the mysterious letters. What he read within made his blood run cold.

"To Mister Prosper Creale, in regard to the trial of your son Clement Creale to answer for charges of espionage against these United States, and treachery against those whom he had sworn to faithfully serve. A true copy of the report offered to his commanding officer is given below.

"Sir, it is my unhappy duty to relay to you the following facts which incriminate the said private soldier Clement Creale. Viz: A letter from his mother, one Kristine Creale, of Charles County, Maryland, in which she urged him to 'follow his sentiments to their inevitable conclusion,' and offered him encouragement in his efforts to 'undermine by whatever means necessary the rebellious officers' under whom he served. She further suggested to him that he could redeem himself with the 'proper rulers of this nation' by taking note of and reporting 'all dispositions and conditions of the rebellious forces.' This said letter was enclosed in one from his father, one Prosper Creale, a known associate of that notorious opponent of American independence, the Anglican preacher Freeborn Garrettson. While the letter from the accused's father contained nothing of obvious import, it is possible that it contained a cipher whose meaning we could not penetrate. Taken together, these letters were incriminating enough that when they were examined in the ordinary course of managing the correspondence of our soldiers, and it was decided that the said private soldier Clement Creale ought to be subjected to questioning. This questioning yielded no results, and it was determined that for the safety of the regiment, its subject ought be confined in solitude within the nearest gaol until such time as we could satisfy ourselves as to the loyalties of his family. This having been arranged, we are now directed to complete our investigation before the disposition of the said Clement Creale may be further considered.

"This record is conveyed to you by way of alerting you to expect an interview with your local Committee of Observation at their earliest convenience, with the object of determining whether you are loyal to the state of Maryland and its representatives in the Congress, or whether you must be regarded as enemies residing within its territory, and subject to the sanctions required under law for the same.

"I am, Sir, your obedient &c., &c.

"Richard Jameson, Esq."

Having hardly breathed the entire time that he devoured the shocking letter, Prosper now felt his breath come in short, labored gasps as he called out, "Wife, come here at once."

She bustled in from the kitchen, a cleaning cloth over one shoulder. He could see her take in his dead white visage as she asked, concern and fear in her voice, "What is the matter, husband?"

He said nothing, but only handed her the letter. She, too, turned pale, clutching at her mouth in horror as she read. When she put the letter aside and sat heavily in the chair at his desk, he asked in a low, deadly quiet voice, "What is the meaning of these things that you wrote to our son?"

"I- I thought that our correspondence was private, and I was only trying to guide him to conducting himself in a manner that would not bring him shame in the years to come, once this foolish rebellion has been brought to heel."

Prosper stared at her in open disbelief, but she continued, doggedly. "I understand that young men can be caught up in the excitement of events that they cannot fully understand, and it was my hope that he would not so far commit himself as to destroy his prospects of an honorable life in the wake of these awful days."

He said nothing to his wife, willing his lungs to continue taking in the breath of life for another few moments while he tried to understand what this woman had done to their son, whether by malicious intent or ignorant accident.

He examined her as he might a stranger and saw for the first time the hardness around her eyes, which revealed a conviction that she was absolutely in the right in her actions. There was anger, too, though he was unsure whether it was directed at their son and his supposed disloyalty to the King, toward Prosper for what new reason he could not imagine, or toward those who had discovered her letter.

He also saw the creeping signs of age in the graying hair that escaped from the edges of her mob cap, and the lines that marked her frown in its accustomed pull on her face.

She averted her face from his gaze suddenly, crying out, "Why are you looking at me like that, husband? I have done no wrong, yet you are inspecting me as though I am a common criminal, delivered up into your study."

Through clenched teeth, "Wife, your ill-considered words have placed our son in jeopardy of his life, and our entire family under a cloud of suspicion. I know you did not agree with Clement's decision to go and fight for our independence, but once he took that decision, you were absolutely obliged to stand aside and permit him to pursue it without interference."

He closed his eyes and shook his head before reopening them to glare down at her. "The rebellion against the Crown is a matter beyond our individual control, but suggesting that Clement ought to seek to undermine it, that he should betray the oaths he has taken and give direct aid to the enemies of this nation — why, I should be surprised if the Committee of Observation does not seize up our property and sell it by means of punishment for your treachery."

She started to speak, and he said, sharply, "No. You must say nothing further until I have had an opportunity to see what our poor son has written, and what this other item may be."

He quickly opened Clement's letter, but it clearly dated from before the awful events outlined in the official's letter had unfolded. It was full of the ordinary reassurances to them both about the conditions in the regimental encampment, greetings to his siblings, and hopeful declarations that the enemy was in retreat everywhere. Prosper set it aside carefully, realizing that it might be the last letter he would ever see from his son.

He broke the seal on the second letter from an unknown hand and read it aloud.

"To Mister Prosper Creale of Charles County, Maryland, and his wife Kristine. Know ye by these presents that your appearance is commanded and required at the hour of ten o'clock in the forenoon on the seventeenth instant before the Committee of Observation, at the courthouse in Port Tobacco Town. If you should fail to respond to these summons, be warned that the Committee will take note of your absence and will find against you in the inquiry it is conducting."

He tossed the page down onto the desk with the other letters. The seventeenth was the very next day. "We must travel tomorrow morning at the break of dawn to be present at the appointed hour. I expect you to be dressed and ready to depart at that time. I do not want to lay eyes upon you before then. Leave me alone now."

He watched her stand leave, containing herself until she passed through the doorway, where he saw her bury her face in her hands as she turned and ran up the stairs. If he had been told that morning that he could direct words of such cold fury to any other living being, Prosper would have been shocked and horrified, but under the circumstances, he felt as though he had exercised remarkable restraint.

In just a few brief lines of a letter that he now remonstrated with himself for not having looked over, Kristine might have undone everything that generations of his family had labored to achieve. He could think of no defense that would satisfy the fervent patriots of the Committee of Observation, and it seemed inevitable that this comfortable house and what remained of his land would be ripped away.

What, then, would become of them? He sat heavily in his chair and uttered a hoarse bark of laughter at the sudden thought that perhaps he could prevail upon Cain to offer him and the children shelter, if they lost their own home. The great cabin he had nearly finished would scarcely fit so many, but it would be better than asking for the charity of their neighbors.

And what of Kristine? Could he ever again trust her as a helpmeet, as a mother to their children, when she had so rashly endangered their son, making it appear that his loyalty was in question? Hers, he had known, was not to the rebellion, but he had not understood the depth of her feeling for the faraway King. And how much of that was genuine regard for the Crown, as opposed to a simple reaction to the cause that had taken her son away from her?

But, if that were the case, why would she place his head in a noose by suggesting that he should "report all dispositions and conditions of the rebellious forces" to the British?

He could make no sense of her actions. His own association with the misrepresented Mister Garrettson, he could explain to the Committee, and he would gladly enough sign any oath of loyalty that they asked of him to demonstrate that he was his own man, and that his religious convictions did not interfere with his political persuasions.

Would they demand the same of a woman? If they did, would Kristine submit, for the sake of their son's safety? And even if she did, what were her true convictions? It almost seemed as though his wife of these many years was a person he knew nothing of, and that revelation shook him almost as deeply as any other aspect of this entire terrible episode.

What kind of future could he envision with a wife who had so shattered their lives? Even if he did somehow manage to retain his plantation, what would it take for him to be able to stand the sight of her again, without remembering those potentially fatal lines from her pen?

The smell of smoke yanked him out of his ruminations, and he leaped up from his desk, dashing into the kitchen. There, he saw at once that a kettle hung on a crane over the flames, with smoke pouring out of it, mostly up the flue, but there was enough that it was drifting out into the house, as well.

He grabbed an iron hook from beside the hearth and drew the kettle away from the hottest part of the fire, being cautious to leave it so that the smoke would continue up the chimney. Things were bad enough without rendering the house unfit for habitation. Whatever had been in the kettle was now a ruined, blackened mass, and he could not help but think that it was somehow a physical manifestation of the condition of his life.

He turned away from the hearth to find Kristine at the doorway, her now-uncovered hair in complete disarray, her face a blotchy red from sobbing, and her nose still streaming. She was panting from having run back down the stairs, and their eyes met for a brief moment before he looked away. In her gaze, he saw utter sorrow, but also a desperate question.

Pushing past her, he returned to his study and closed the door firmly.

Chapter 21

The ride to the courthouse where the Committee of Observation met promised to be the longest, most uncomfortable several hours that Prosper could ever recall having endured. He had refused to acknowledge Kristine, other than to motion her into the back of the cart, rather than her accustomed seat beside him in the front.

He knew that the jostling of the road was worse in back, but he had only become more and more furious with her as the sleepless night had progressed. The utter gall of a woman, with no understanding of the complexities of the world, bringing both his legacy and their son to the brink of extinction with just a few lines of her pen! It made him grit his teeth all over again to think of it.

He was no kinder to himself, though. If he had only read over her pages — had so much as glanced at them — he might have been able to intercept their potentially deadly message, as well as giving her an education as to the forces she was toying with through her words. For that matter, if he had engaged her in a more considered discussion of her views, he might have been able to persuade her of the faults in her reasoning.

What time he had not spent in self-recrimination, he had spent in prayer. At one point, he had lit a taper and turned to the Psalms. "My God, my God, why hast thou forsaken me? Why art thou so far from helping me, and from the words of my roaring? O my God, I cry in the daytime, but thou hearest not; and in the night season, and am not silent."

Reading on, he found that he was weeping by the end of the infamous passage, the one that Christ Himself had cited in his hour of greatest suffering. "Oh, blessed Lord, let this be the moment of my greatest suffering, and not merely a preparation for the greater sorrow to come," he murmured fervently.

Unlike that spring day when heard the voice of the Lord, now that Prosper needed most to hear a reassuring word in his ear, God was silent, leaving him to carry his bitter and terror-filled burden alone.

Snuffing the candle, he laid his Bible back down and returned to his bed, wondering anew whether he should not have turned instead to Job for comfort, but it seemed a blasphemy even now to compare his trials with those visited upon that great and holy man. After all, Prosper could not claim to be as upright and perfect a man as Job was described, even before God favored him with His direct guidance.

"Naked came I out of my mother's womb, and naked shall I return thither: the Lord gave, and the Lord hath taken away." If the worst came to pass, could Prosper behave in any way other than according to the example of Job, mourning the earthly losses in his life in the earthly fashion, but yet praying to God in gratitude for what he had been granted?

Yet, what to make of Kristine's role in all of this, and what had guided her actions? Had she been acting as an unwitting tool of Satan in contributing to Prosper's tribulations?

Or was Prosper the author of his own trials, whether he had done the right thing by following the word of God, or had erred in some fashion as he had sought to understand it? If he had not freed his slaves, would Clement have felt moved to volunteer for the Continental Army? Would Kristine have written to their son with such terrible advice, even if the young man had felt moved to join up?

Had everything gone wrong for him when he had heard the voice of God that spring, setting into motion a chain of events that would bring him to stand before the Committee? He rolled over and pulled his cap over his eyes, trying to blot out the external signs of a world that seemed to offer him no avenue for success, and which might, indeed, deny him even the option of mere survival.

When sleep finally did overtake him, it was almost immediately interrupted by an unbidden vision of a body swinging from a gallows, dancing its last as the rope arrested its fall. He had hastily arisen and relit the taper, seeking refuge in whatever passage the Lord might choose to guide his hand to.

Even the confusion and unease of Revelation would be an improvement over such visions as the devil must have sent to his sleeping mind. The details of the Lord's commandments to Moses, enumerating the many offerings that were asked of the children of Israel, formed a comfortably numbing barrier against the return of the awful jerk and twitch that his mind replayed repeatedly at any moment when it was not occupied with God's word.

The minutiae of one verse after another were a tiny salvation as the late hours of the night crawled into the early hours of the morning, and it became time to rise, dress, and prepare the cart for their ride in separate silence over the noisy roads.

They passed through the village early enough that hardly anyone was stirring. The sun still lay just below the horizon, streaking the sky with a riotous cacophony of crimson and orange as daybreak approached.

They passed the home of the old herbalist, Missus Grant, and Prosper groaned inwardly to see that she was already out in her garden, a basket slung over one arm as she selected just the right flowers to harvest for some cure or another.

She looked up at the sound of the cart, and her wave of greeting was cut short by a perplexed frown as she took note of Kristine's form huddled against the back of Prosper's seat, in the body of the cart.

She stepped out of her garden and into the road, forcing Prosper to rein in the horse and stop in front of her.

Her angry demand likewise stopped him in his tracks. "What is the meaning of this, Prosper Creale, driving along with your wife in the back of the cart as though she was so much produce on the way to market?"

He looked down at her and was still formulating a reply when Kristine spoke up from behind him. "It is no worse than I deserve, Livinia, for I have, in my ignorance and spite, most likely cost our family our home, our livelihood, and our son."

Prosper turned in his seat to stare at his wife in open wonder. Her face was streaked with the tracks of tears through the dust that had already darkened it, and her eyes brimmed again with a fresh addition.

Missus Grant spoke gently to her now. "Oh, Kristine, how could it possibly be as terrible as that? I know you to be a careful and loving steward of all of that which you claim to have destroyed."

Having had a moment to consider what he'd seen in

Kristine's eyes, Prosper said, "Missus Grant, even a careful steward can suffer a moment of poor judgment, and in these dangerous days, it takes no more than that to accomplish terrible harm. Still, you are correct in observing that it is not right for me to force my wife to suffer our journey in this fashion."

He turned to Kristine and sighed. "Wife, you should join me in the front, both because it is your proper place, and because I am making a needless spectacle of you before your neighbors in my own spite and ignorance."

He addressed Missus Grant again. "We shall have enough of spectacle by and by, if this day's events go as I fear they will."

She favored him with a deep frown. "I confess that I do not have any idea what you speak of, Mister Creale."

"We are to go before the Committee of Observation and defend ourselves today against charges of treachery against this state, and to present what evidence we can to exonerate our son from charges of the same and worse against the Continental Army."

If anything, the herbalist's frown deepened. "I had heard that Clement had joined up of his own accord, and I find it utterly beyond belief that he should have acted to betray what he had believed in so fervently that he was willing to put his life and health at risk to defend it. What has raised the specter of such grave charges against such an upright young man?"

Prosper found himself explaining the whole sorry affair to the woman, and was unsurprised when she finally scoffed, "What a bunch of nonsense they have raised, out of an innocent comment from a mother to a son."

Kristine spoke up again. "It was not wholly innocent, in fact. I did desire him to make use of his position in the Maryland

Regiment to undermine the success of the Continental forces in the field against the King's men. And I did set forth that desire on paper, not realizing that my letters could be read by any number of people along the way to my son."

She glanced at Prosper for a moment, and then continued. "I have repented of these views upon much reflection and prayer throughout the night since we received word of Clement's imprisonment and our own coming trial. Not just because of the awful consequences," she added quickly, "but because I came to understand that my duty as a mother is to give my son encouragement in the pursuit of what he believes, and not to suggest ways in which he might change those beliefs."

She hung her head. "I have failed in my responsibilities as a helpmeet and as a mother, and I only pray that the good Lord will see fit to forgive me, and to guide the authorities on Earth to do likewise."

Standing and jumping heavily off the back of the cart, she walked around and climbed up beside Prosper. "We must be on our way, so as not to be late to our appointed time before the Committee, Missus Grant, but I thank you for your concern."

The herbalist said, "I will pray for your deliverance from these terrible times, my friends." She stood aside to permit Prosper to urge the horse back into motion.

The sun had risen fully as they had spoken with Missus Grant, and Prosper had to shade his eyes. With his hand concealing his gaze, he looked at his wife, who now slumped against her side of the seat, her eyes closed, and tears trickling down her face.

He realized that he had been terribly unjust to her the prior evening, and all through the night and morning until their encounter with Missus Grant. Yes, she had made an awful mistake, but mere creatures of clay were born to make mistakes, and still their Creator forgave them. Her error had been one born of care and concern, not wickedness, nor even spite, and he had been wrong to think otherwise.

The cost of sin was eternal damnation, but by merely accepting the salvation offered by the Lord, any sinner could be washed clean of his mistakes. Could a husband offer any less to his wife when she confessed her error and accepted responsibility for the consequences?

And would he not stand taller before the Committee of Observation if he stood in union with her, and not in opposition? This Committee did not consist of angels, after all, nor even saints, but mere men like himself, and who among them could have failed to fall into some form of grievous fault at some point in their lives?

Could they not be relied upon to understand and forgive such a transgression when it was recanted and repented? He glanced over again at Kristine and realized that her face had relaxed now into the softness of sleep, and he permitted himself to hope for the first time since he had read yesterday's terrible letter.

Chapter 22

Prosper watched a dust mote dance in the air, lit by a beam of morning sunlight streaming in through the window. He and Kristine had arrived early — or else the Committee was running late — and they had been directed to wait on the bench outside the courtroom where meetings were held.

After she had woken up under a blazing morning sun, he and Kristine had discussed many things along the journey, but most of all, forgiving one another for the many mis-steps and incomplete understandings that had led them to this point. She had, quite fairly, pointed out that he was not always good about explaining his rationales for the actions he took, and that this trait had been particularly marked since he had begun attending Mister Garrettson's sermons.

Left without information from which she could come to informed opinions, she admitted that she had been more inclined toward whatever ran contrary to his actions, if only out of stubborn resentment. She said that she now understood that this had led her into sin and error, and she prayed that it would not cost them dearly.

For his part, Prosper told her that he had fallen out of the habit of consulting her at least in part because he was weary of her reflexive opposition to change, no matter how justified or essential. As it was, ultimately, his responsibility to make decisions for the household, he had retreated to the less time-consuming process of simply making them alone.

Not a few tears had been shed on both sides of the wagon's bench, and as they pulled up before the courthouse, Prosper felt certain that, whatever happened, he and Kristine would find a way to weather it together. Now, watching dust float through a sunbeam, he held her hand in silence as they waited.

He could hear movement beyond the heavy door to the courtroom, and he could only presume that the Committee was arriving through some private entrance and getting ready for the business of the day. Once again, he reminded himself that they were just men, not unlike himself in any significant degree, for all that they held the power to ruin him in the very palms of their hands.

The door opened abruptly, and Prosper felt Kristine jump slightly beside him. A neatly-dressed boy emerged and called out, far more loudly than was necessary, "Are Prosper Creale and his wife Kristine present in the building as required by a letter transmitted to them on the fifteenth day of this month?"

Prosper rose, pulling Kristine to her feet beside him. "Aye, we are here."

"Follow me, then." The boy hardly even looked to see whether they were, in fact, following him but re-entered the courtroom, his posture emanating boredom. To him, this proceeding was obviously just another in an endless series of such dull affairs, rather than representing the possible change of the entire course of a man's life.

Prosper kept his sour thoughts out of his expression, though, as they entered the room. Seated at the front of the room was an assemblage of eight men, all but one of whom looked up in curiosity as the couple walked up the aisle toward them. The exception was a man at the center of the group, who was reading over a page on the desk before him.

Finally, he looked up from his desk. "Mister and Missus Creale, I presume?"

Prosper said, in a voice that he was surprised did not reveal the quaver he felt within, "Yes, sir."

"Very good. Thank you for your punctuality. You would be surprised at how many people fail to observe that basic courtesy to this Committee. I am Josias Hawkins, and I hold the chair of this Committee of Observation today. I will permit the other members of the Committee to introduce themselves as they have occasion to ask you any questions, all right?"

"Yes, sir." This time, Prosper could hear the quaver, and it filled him with shame to be so intimidated by a man whom he judged to be of an age with himself, and with little in his appearance to distinguish his station as being any different from that which Prosper held in their community.

"Have a seat, both of you," Hawkins said. His tone was not harsh, but neither was it kind.

Without further preamble, he held up the page that he had been consulting. "We have here a report from the First Maryland Regiment, that your son, a private soldier in that regiment by the name of Clement, received from your hand a letter that raised certain questions about his purpose for having joined that military unit."

"So I understand," said Prosper. "And what I have heard of that letter, I understand the concerns that it raised."

"What you have heard of the letter?" The official seemed incredulous. "Did you not dispatch the letter through the post, then?"

"I did," Prosper said, "But I did not pen the portions which have caused so much trouble."

Hawkins' eyebrows rose to the severe edge of the hair that hung over his forehead, and Prosper felt Kristine stir beside him. She spoke up, her voice firm and steady. "I wrote the portions that raised the questions, through a combination of motherly concern for a son whose decisions I did not fully understand, and an uninformed opinion of the causes and state of our contest with the English crown. I have lately become acquainted with the error of my ways and am prepared to fully and forever recant anything that may have given offense or concern to either civil authority or military."

She sat upright, her bearing something like regal, while still managing to look contrite in her facial expression.

Prosper had never loved her more than he did in that instant, but he turned away from examining her to see what he could judge of the Committee's reaction to her words.

Hawkins looked startled, but thoughtful, and one of the men to the far end of the panel was whispering something into the ear of the man beside him. The rest of the men's faces bore expressions that ranged from dubious to impressed, save for one man whose brows were lowered in obvious irritation.

That man spoke up now, saying, "I am Warren Dent, merchant in this town. Mister Creale, are you in the habit of permitting your wife to speak out of turn, particularly in a gathering such as this?"

Prosper said, without hesitation, "Mister Dent, as we are here based on her having written on her own accord, I do not think it inappropriate that she ought speak on her own accord."

Mister Dent frowned, but nodded, admitting, "Fairly put, sir."

Clearing his throat, Mister Hawkins said, "I believe that under the circumstances, Mister Creale's position is correct, and that we can stand to hear from his wife without his intercession. If I may address myself directly to her, sir?"

Prosper nodded, and Hawkins continued, "Missus Creale, while we do not of routine ask for oaths of loyalty from women in our community, may I presume that you would have no objection to swearing one such, if it were asked of you?"

"No objection whatever, sir," she said.

He nodded in satisfaction and looked around to the other members of the Committee. The men who had been whispering to each other at the end of the row both leaned forward to catch Hawkins' eye, and he motioned to the closer one first. "Go ahead, Mister Turner, and we'll come to you next, Mister Brown."

Turner faced Kristine and bowed slightly in his seat. "Missus Creale, I am Zephaniah Turner, also a merchant of this town. I mean absolutely no disrespect when I ask this, but having read an excerpt of the letter that you addressed to your son, duty compels me to ask you what possessed you to believe that you could offer such advice to a man grown? Do you not know your place in this world, madam?"

Without giving her a chance to answer — Prosper thought that this was probably a good thing, feeling how she had stiffened beside him — the man turned his attention now to him. "And

Mister Creale, I am likewise astonished, sir, that you should have so rashly permitted your wife to include such lines as these in a letter that you then sent onward to your son, undermining both his steadfast zeal for our country and the security of his position in its service."

Prosper stared at the man in disbelief for a long moment, unable to formulate an answer that would not have been disastrous. He was rescued by Mister Hawkins, who asked dryly, "Had you a question for either of them, Zeph, or are you just making speeches again?"

Turner scowled, but muttered, "I have heard all I need hear from them," and sat back.

Hawkins nodded and said, "Doctor Brown, what have you to add to Mister Turner's observations, or did you have questions?"

"I had only a minor inquiry to add to your own, sir." Turning to Prosper, he introduced himself. "Gustavus Brown, doctor of medicine, at your service. Sir, your wife has said that she would have no objection to swearing loyalty to this state and to our independent nation. I am aware that some of your Anglican brethren have objected in principle to the swearing of oaths, and I should like to assure myself that you do not so object."

Prosper said, briskly, "I would be happy to swear loyalty, Doctor Brown. I do not hold with all the feelings of my brethren, and indeed, have lately broken with certain of them over particular questions of how we must observe the will of our blessed Lord."

Doctor Brown pursed his lips thoughtfully, and said, "On another occasion, I should be most curious to discuss these questions with you, if only as an observer of the human condition and of our various means of understanding our relationship with the great

Author of the world. No further questions, Mister Hawkins."

Hawkins glanced around to the rest of the Committee once more, and then said, "You may both go back outside and await our decision. Again, I personally thank you for the courtesy of your punctuality."

Prosper and Kristine stood and were led back into the hallway by the boy, who closed the door behind them with a heavy, muffled thud. Prosper exchanged a look with his wife, and they went back to the bench to sit down again and await their fate.

Chapter 23

The single dust mote from earlier had been joined by a multitude of others now, as the room warmed up in the lengthening morning. Prosper watched them dance, illustrating the currents in the air made when a man passed through the hallway, paying no attention to the couple sitting on the hard bench, awaiting their fate.

The stranger disappeared into a door at the far end of the hall, and in the noise made when he closed the door behind himself, he did not hear the courtroom door open. The boy was standing in the doorway, an expectant expression on his face, when Prosper looked back in his direction, and he felt Kristine jump slightly beside him as she, too, was startled by the boy's appearance.

Prosper found his voice and asked, "Are we to return to the Committee's chambers so soon?"

The boy looked at him with what he thought was a hint of scornfulness, and replied, "Yes, that is why I am waiting here for you."

Prosper and Kristine rose in unison, and she followed her husband back into the courtroom. He could not help but think that the boy's apparent disdain for them augured poorly for the Committee's decision, and he felt a clutch of fear in his chest.

Already, his mind was racing through the possibilities of how they would get through the next few days, the next fortnight, the coming months, if they were truly to be dispossessed of their plantation. Who might take in their large family? What would become of the field hands without him there to fulfill the agreement he had made with them?

Cain's cabin was unlikely to be large enough to accommodate them all. That assumed that the man would even be willing to take them in. The children he could spread across a few friends' homes. Perhaps Mister Stone would be kind enough to house him and his wife.

The hands would have to fend for themselves, he thought in the last moments before he and Kristine reached their former seats before the Committee, though he would surely put in a good word for them with whoever acquired the plantation. Perhaps they would be permitted to continue working it while the process wound its way to completion? That might at least preserve the value of the current growing season.

These thoughts were interrupted by Mister Hawkins clearing his throat as they sat. "I trust that you were not too discomfited by the delay while we came to a decision, Mister Creale."

"No, sir," said Prosper, wanting to dispense with the niceties and get on to the business at hand.

Hawkins picked up a page from his desk and consulted it as he began to speak. "Very good. By a majority of six members in favor and two opposed, the Committee of Observation has concluded we are satisfied as to Missus Creale's loyalty and your own to the cause of American independence. You are cautioned to strictly avoid any appearance of opposition to the Continental Congress, the Maryland Convention, or this Committee, lest we should be forced to again take up consideration of the question of your loyalty."

Prosper could hear a roaring in his ears as relief washed over him, as sharp and distinct as if someone had dashed a bucket of cold seawater upon him. Mister Hawkins was still speaking, though, and he forced himself to focus on the man's words.

"We are, as a majority, persuaded that Missus Creale's letter was, as she testified, written out of matronly concern for the well-being of her son, and not as the continuation of a plot to which he was a party to undermine the security and effectiveness of the Continental Army. As a result, we will dispatch at once a letter to his commanding officer expressing our opinion that he should no longer be held on suspicion of treason and espionage."

He frowned and hesitated, as though unwilling to continue, but then visibly forced himself to finish. "Sadly, we cannot promise that military authority will take any notice of our findings, so it would be most desirable for you to transmit at once correspondence making clear your understanding of the error you committed and proclaiming your loyalty to their cause. A court-martial, should he be subjected to such, operates under its own rules and customs, and you would be well-advised to seek the counsel of someone more intimately acquainted with them than are most of us."

Hawkins put down the page and said, mildly, "You are free to go about your lawful business, although Doctor Brown has expressed a wish to speak with you, if you can make yourself available to him."

Prosper stood abruptly, and his wife followed him to her feet. "I thank God and this Committee for the mercy you have shown us. I should be most happy to speak with Doctor Brown, now or at any time."

Doctor Brown nodded and said, "I shall accompany you and your wife out of the chamber, sir, if you please." He stood and walked around the line of desks, getting a sour look from Mister Turner as he passed. Prosper felt certain that he knew where one of the two votes against him had come from.

The doctor took his elbow and led Prosper back out of the main door of the courtroom, saying quietly to him once they reached the hallway, "You have been through an ordeal today, sir, and I believe that it may not be taken amiss were I to offer you both some refreshment before you begin your journey back home."

Prosper smiled at the man with sincere gratitude. "We should both be most obliged, Doctor. It has, indeed, been a very trying day, and we have some hours on the road ahead of us before it is concluded."

"Of course. Just come this way, and I will have some tea brought around, and perhaps a plate of some cold pastries? I assure you that it is no trouble at all, as I believe that my cook has them prepared already for my morning tea. Or should you prefer something more fortifying? A punch, perhaps, or cider?"

"Tea would be quite welcome, Doctor," said Kristine. "With a trip still ahead of us today, we should keep our wits undulled, I think."

"My wife speaks quite rightly," Prosper said, as the doctor led them single file up a narrow back stairway.

At the top, where it opened into a hallway that mirrored the one on the ground floor, Doctor Brown led them to the first doorway, and opened it for them, motioning for them to precede him inside. They found themselves in a small, well-appointed room,

with comfortable chairs around a small table. It was evidently
a room intended for legal conferences or similar gatherings, and
Prosper found that it intimidated him ever so slightly.

Once the couple took their seats beside each other at the
table, Doctor Brown leaned back out of the door and called out,
"Richard, can you have Sara bring around morning tea for three,
as quickly as ever she can?" Prosper could hear a high, thin voice
answer indistinctly, and the doctor nodded, seeming satisfied, and
came into the room to sit across from them.

"As you must know, your religious activities formed no
small part of the reason for suspicion against you, and I am sorry
for that part of your troubles," he said, settling himself into the
chair. "However, I found that I was intrigued by your passing
reference to certain differences that you have with the leaders of
your faith. Would you care to elaborate upon those?"

"Certainly," Prosper said, overcoming his unease as he
felt the satisfaction of the opportunity to discuss the Gospel with
someone eager to hear what he had to say. He laid out the essentials
of Mister Garrettson's testimony, and then said, "That wasn't the
thing that persuaded me in the end, however."

"Oh? What, then?"

"God spoke to me directly, and he placed directly in my
ear the words of the Gospel of Luke, chapter 12, verse 48. Do you
happen to recall that verse, Doctor?"

Doctor Brown shook his head. "I was never much of a
memorizer of the Bible," he confessed.

"Unto whomsoever much is given, of him shall much be
required. He reminded me, in His own holy words, that I had
benefited mightily from the labors of the men I enslaved, and that

I owed them much compensation for their labor."

He shrugged. "So, I gave them each their manumission, as well as an acre of land free and clear for every year they had spent in my bondage. I cannot claim to have made them whole for the harm inflicted upon them, but I can at least say that I have given them each their due."

Doctor Brown's eyebrows rose almost entirely out of sight beneath his hair, but they were interrupted by a soft knock at the door before he could respond.

"Come in," Doctor Brown called, and a young woman entered, her bleached mob cap and apron a stark contrast against her dark skin. She bore a large silver platter, which had a tea service atop it, and a silver plate covered with delicate-looking pastries.

She set it upon the table and withdrew silently, Doctor Brown's face turning faintly red as she did so. "Er, that was Sara, who is the daughter of my cook. I must confess that I am not as enlightened as are you and Mister Garrettson, nor have I the capacity to make do without house servants."

Prosper dipped his head in acknowledgment of the other man's admission. "God has not yet blessed you with His intercession, and even among those who have heard His word, many resist it. I believe that it is but justice to free our slaves, but you must come to that of your own accord. I will not impose my beliefs on any man."

Kristine broke the somber mood, asking, "Might I sample one of those pastries? They look as though your cook is very skilled indeed."

"Certainly, and I shall pour us each some tea," said Brown, obviously relieved at the change in topic. The conversation turned

to questions of baking technique and praise for the fine tea he served
— "Only the best smuggled bohea," Brown averred — and finally,
Prosper stood.

"I thank you for your hospitality and your willingness to
share fellowship with another seeker of God's will," he said, "but
we have a long ride ahead of us, and I should like to be home before
the hour is too far advanced."

"Of course," Doctor Brown said, rising and brushing
crumbs from his waistcoat. "I give you the joy of your innocence
and the hope of your son's restoration, as well."

"Thank you, doctor," Kristine said, and followed her
husband to the door. "I hope that we shall meet under happier
circumstances at some future time, sir."

"As do I, madam." He escorted them to the door, and
stood there, watching them as they went down the stairs. In the
closeness of the narrow stairwell, the sound of their feet on the
treads the only noise that reached them, Prosper heard a familiar
voice in his ear.

"Peace I leave with you, my peace I give unto you." Prosper
paused for a moment, smiled, and followed Kristine out into the
bright light of the entrance hall.

Epilogue

Prosper paused and leaned against his shovel, sharing a moment of respite with Primus. He could see that the grave was deep enough, and it was time to lower Frankie's plain pine coffin into the ground.

He nodded to Cain and stood back as the man took up his end of a rope in concert with the three other men who had accepted the responsibility of lowering their friend to his final resting place. The years since Prosper had freed him had been kind to the old man, and when the time came, God called him home from a peaceful slumber, finally freed of the aches and pains of a lifetime of hard labor.

As he watched the four men let down their ropes and the coffin sink into the ground, Prosper reflected on the trials that the same years had brought him and his family.

Cleared of suspicion, Clement had been restored to his unit. Although the threat of British incursion into Maryland had never materialized, the First Maryland Regiment was dispatched to New-York to hold the city against the British.

The defense of New-York came to a dramatic end as British forces surrounded the Americans, and from what Prosper had read in breathless accounts printed in newspapers, the outnumbered Maryland regiment distinguished itself by boldly attacking the British, permitting the rest of the American forces to slip away.

General Washington was widely quoted as having said of them, "Good God, what brave fellows I must this day lose!"

Whatever pride Prosper might have felt at Clement's part in such a heroic effort was shattered by the hurried letter he'd received, informing him that his son had been among those whom Washington had lost.

He still couldn't decide what had been the worst part — reading the awful letter, or having to tell Kristine of its contents. Her wild howl of anguish would echo in his memory for all his days, and no prayer to God would relieve the pain that he felt at losing his son, magnified by his wife's pain.

In the awful days that had followed the letter, Prosper had wished that God might speak to him again with some words of comfort, but found that even without any words, he was aware of God's silent presence, and took some solace in the certainty that his son was in the care of his Creator.

His grief had yielded to the everyday demands of ensuring that the hands could bring in a crop, and managing the payment of their salaries from the proceeds of its sale. He took a grim satisfaction in being able to balance his books at the end of the season, and when the following year's crop had been even better, he'd bought Kristine a new dress.

After her initial shock, she had forbade any mention of the war or her son for many months, and on more than one occasion, Prosper had awoken to her sobbing beside him in the night. She surprised him one day by announcing that she was joining a sewing circle with other mothers who had lost sons, and were gathering to make clothing for Continental soldiers.

He was yanked out of his recollections as Cain asked

him, "Would you say some words, Mister Creale?" Prosper had completely missed the coffin reaching the bottom of the grave and the men pulling their ropes free, their companion gently set into place.

He nodded and handed his shovel to Primus. Stooping, he picked up his Bible from the folded jacket he'd set it on while he worked, and opened it to the first passage he'd marked that morning.

Clearing his throat, he said, "I have chosen a passage that I believe our friend Frankie would have appreciated, and I will follow that with one which has been a great comfort to me of late."

He looked down at the page and read carefully, "Hast thou not known? Hast thou not heard, that the everlasting God, the Lord, the Creator of the ends of the earth, fainteth not, neither is weary? There is no searching of his understanding."

Prosper glanced around and took a deep breath before reading on. "He giveth power to the faint; and to them that have no might he increaseth strength. Even the youths shall faint and be weary, and the young men shall utterly fall."

He heard his own voice break as he read the last words of the passage, and was surprised to notice a tear splattering on the page. Gathering himself, he concluded, forcing his reading to be steady and strong, "But they that wait upon the Lord shall renew their strength; they shall mount up with wings as eagles; they shall run and not be weary; and they shall walk, and not faint."

Closing the book, he stood silent for a long moment, listening to the quiet sniffles and Cain's unabashed sobs. Then he nodded, as if to himself, and opened the Bible again to the second passage he had marked.

As he read, he heard a familiar voice speaking the words along with him, and the realization gave his reading fresh strength and clarity.

"Let not your heart be troubled; ye believe in God, believe also in me. In my Father's house are many mansions: if it were not so, I would have told you. I go to prepare a place for you. And if I go and prepare a place for you, I will come again, and receive you unto myself; that where I am, there ye may be also. And whither I go ye know, and the way ye know."

He closed the book again and stood for a while with his eyes closed. Then he looked around at the men who gathered beside the open grave, and said, "Our brother Frankie goes before us, but we all will know the way in our time. He, and all we love, will be waiting for us, with the places our Father has prepared for us. Let our hearts be glad for this knowledge, and comforted in it."

He lowered his head again, and recited now from memory.

"The Lord is my shepherd; I shall not want. He maketh me to lie down in green pastures: he leadeth me beside the still waters. He restoreth my soul: he leadeth me in the paths of righteousness for his name's sake. Yea, though I walk through the valley of the shadow of death, I will fear no evil: for thou art with me; thy rod and thy staff they comfort me. Thou preparest a table before me in the presence of mine enemies: thou anointest my head with oil; my cup runneth over. Surely goodness and mercy shall follow me all the days of my life: and I will dwell in the house of the Lord for ever."

Also in Audiobook

Many readers love the experience of turning the pages in a paper book such as the one you hold in your hands. Others enjoy hearing a skilled narrator tell them a story, bringing the words on the page to life.

Brief Candle Press has arranged to have *The Word* produced as a high-quality audiobook, and you can listen to a sample and learn where to purchase it in that form by scanning the QR code below with your phone, tablet, or other device, or going to the Web address shown.

Happy listening!

tfar.us/TheWordAudio

Historical Notes

Readers of my novels *The Light* and *The Path* will already be familiar with the Quaker roots of the abolitionist movement, but I was surprised to encounter a wholly separate thread of its origins in the early evangelical Methodist church.

Freeborn Garrettson was a leader of this Christian response to slavery, and the account in this novel of the reasons behind his decision to free his slaves is drawn almost verbatim from his own discussion of it in the fine 1829 biography *The Life of the Rev. Freeborn Garrettson*, by Nathan Bangs. I found independent accounts of his congregants being inspired to follow suit, and so I chose to tell the story from that point of view.

The history of slavery in this nation is awful and particularly pungent in the era of the American War of Independence. Men who cried out the loudest for liberty denied its blessings to their own slaves, and even if they acknowledged this dissonance, they excused themselves by claiming that the men and women kidnapped from Africa were somehow less human than their European captors.

It is one of the enduring frustrations of all students of early American history who must grapple with it, and there is no satisfactory explanation for it.

I have dealt with the problem of slavery in the Revolutionary era before now — most notably in *The Freedman* — but I decided that it was time to get down in the mud with it and wrestle with it on its own turf. That said, I have undoubtedly been too kind to the men and women who presumed to own other human beings, and my disgust with the practice of slavery is greater than with any other single fact of the Revolution.

In addition to the Reverend Garrettson, the other real people in my novel are the members of the Committee of Observation for Charles County, Maryland. Of the several dozen members of the Committee (any seven of whom could meet to discharge its responsibilities), I picked several names more or less at random, and wound up encountering some delightful minor historical figures.

Zephaniah Turner, I discovered, wrote a letter to President Washington in 1789, proposing that each state be strictly limited to no more than two practicing attorneys at law. From this letter, I developed a sketch of a man who might have confronted Kristine and Prosper with the sort of noxious comments I've put in his mouth. No disrespect was intended toward him, but his letter does make for entertaining reading.

Gustavus Brown was an even more interesting historical figure. As I've depicted, he was a physician, and in fact, was one of the physicians attending George Washington on the night of the former President's death. There was no way, of course, to foreshadow that in my book, but I did feel drawn to give him a somewhat larger role than he might otherwise have gotten.

Maryland's First Regiment, as described, went into history at the Battle of Long Island as the "Maryland 400" for their incredible sacrifice. Attacking a vastly superior British force, they charged at the enemy line repeatedly until all but a dozen were dead or captured. Their actions saved the rest of the Continental

Army and they are credited with averting the failure of the entire Revolution in that battle.

A short note about the names I gave to the Creale family members. While they were Anglicans, and members of the nascent Methodist church, I imagined that they must have had family roots in the Puritan movement, where the sort of "virtue names" I've bestowed on them were a common practice. It was meant as a nod to the sorts of family traditions that so many of us follow, long after the meaning behind them has been lost.

Acknowledgements

Writing a novel with characters of such deep faith as we see in the pages of this book was a unique challenge, and I want to acknowledge the very kind review of my depiction of early Methodist theology by Jennifer Lane, whose background as a native Marylander and a student of the early Methodist movement gave her insights that I could not hope to match.

In addition, my friend Lia London offered many insightful and useful comments, which greatly improved the story in both its details and in its structure.

Any errors or misstatements of the details of the theology I depict in this novel, of course, remain my own.